**monsoon**books

## HARVESTING THE STORM

John Waromi was born in 1960 in West Papua, Indonesia. After studying law at Cenderawasih University, he moved to Jakarta and joined Indonesia's most famous dramatic troupe, Rendra's Bengkel Teater. As an actor he performed throughout Indonesia as well as touring New York, Japan and Korea. John was invited to the Ubud Writers & Readers Festival, followed closely by an invitation to the Balinale International Film Festival, also in Bali, and the Northern Territory Writers Festival, in Darwin, Australia. He now lives and writes in his home province.

# Harvesting the Storm

John Waromi

Translated by
Sarita Newson

**monsoonbooks**

Published in 2019
by Monsoon Books Ltd
www.monsoonbooks.co.uk

No.1 Duke of Windsor Suite, Burrough Court,
Burrough on the Hill, Leics. LE14 2QS, UK.

ISBN (paperback): 978-1-912049-48-6
ISBN (ebook): 978-1-912049-49-3

First published in Indonesian in 2014 as "Anggadi Tupa"
by the Lontar Foundation in cooperation with Saritaksu Editions.
Copyright in the English language translation © 2014 Sarita Newson.
Copyright in the English language edition © 2014 The Lontar
Foundation and Saritaksu Editions.

Copyright©John Waromi, 2014.

The moral right of the author has been asserted.

All rights reserved. No part of this publication may be reproduced,
stored in a retrieval system, or transmitted, in any form or by any
means without the prior written permission of the publisher, nor be
otherwise circulated in any form of binding or cover other than that in
which it is published and without a similar condition being imposed on
the subsequent purchaser.

Cover design by Sukutangan.

A Cataloguing-in-Publication data record is available from the British
Library.

Printed and bound in Great Britain by Clays Ltd, Elcograf S.p.A.
21 20 19      1 2 3 4 5

For Rabasanei, and my father daii Ambab

*If you're afraid of the tide,
don't make your home on the shore*

Frans Maror

# Contents

| | |
|---|---|
| MAIN CHARACTERS | 13 |
| Prologue | 15 |
| Greedy | 17 |
| The Tragedy | 24 |
| Andevavait's Sacrifice | 27 |
| A Bamboo-cutting Ritual | 31 |
| Contemplating Fate | 36 |
| The Village Under the Moon | 41 |
| The Risks of Hunting | 45 |
| Initiation and Karma | 58 |
| Living on the Sea Shore | 60 |
| Mandohi Pastoral | 65 |
| Personal Naivety | 70 |
| The Sower of Seeds | 74 |
| Magic of the Morning Star | 79 |
| Night Mystery | 81 |
| A Faceless Guest | 84 |
| The Stealing of *Je Anggadi* | 90 |
| A Breath of Tradition | 93 |

| | |
|---|---|
| A Hot Heart | 96 |
| Masterpiece | 101 |
| Seven Rainbows | 105 |
| Mystery Cave | 108 |
| Balance | 110 |
| The Arrival of Good Luck | 113 |
| Adventure | 118 |
| Trapped | 122 |
| Contemplation | 126 |
| The Triumvirate of Sound | 131 |
| A Tale of Viami | 136 |
| Nature's Forbidden List | 141 |
| The Benefactor | 144 |
| A Quiet Moment | 146 |
| Mangga-maraing and the Boiling Water | 153 |
| Amidst a Thousand Islands | 155 |
| The Early Feast | 159 |
| Prince of the Sun | 163 |
| We-dobarai: the Last Party | 165 |
| A Legacy of Pearls | 171 |
| O Butterfly | 177 |
| Antarawihi, the Magic Leaf | 180 |
| The Power of Airokung | 185 |
| Tentamu – Absolute Perfection | 190 |
| Inov the Poisonous Stonefish | 193 |
| Epilogue | 195 |

| | |
|---|---|
| KAMPONG VIETNAM AND ITS HISTORIC BACKGROUND | 199 |
| SAPURIWAN | 207 |
| GLOSSARY OF AMBAI WORDS | 209 |
| IN REMEMBRANCE OF THE BOMB VICTIMS | 219 |
| BOOKS BY INDONESIAN AUTHORS | 224 |
| BOOKS SET IN INDONESIA | 224 |

# Main Characters

**(In order of appearance)**

Andevavait, the amphibious tidepool blenny
Bohurai, the toadfish
Anggereai, the striped crab
Raukahi, the octopus
Andawai, the red-lined triggerfish

# Prologue

A child calls out as he runs along the beach. '*Aii yee, Daiiee!* Mama, Papa! *Anggadi tupa, anggadi tupa!* The coconuts are coming! The coconuts are coming!'

A man in the distance replies, echoing his call.

'*Tafu ee!* Grandma, Grandpa! *Anggadi tupa, anggadi tupa!* The coconuts are coming! The coconuts are coming!'

A woman appears from the same direction. She stops and stares at them.

Suddenly, they appear through the gaps in the reef. The dark wet shapes float and roll in the whitewash of the waves as they are eventually cast ashore.

The boy and his father scramble for them. They will plant coconuts all along the shore.

One by one the names of the fishes are called out loud, and they are imprinted upon the child's memory. One by one the father calls out the plant names, and the boy commits them to memory. All the names, that is, except that of *anggadi*, the coconut.

... all the plants that grow and bloom in the ocean.

... all the plants that grow and bear fruit.

Even those that grow in spirals, climbing, blooming and

bearing fruit on the trees.

Their leaves are full of life, they have a voice, and they talk, whisper and sing.

Their skin sweats, feels, touches, smells, listens and sees.

There are reptiles of all shapes and sizes; some without hands and feet, others with lots of feet – some with as many as eight feet plus a pair of hands, four feet and no hands, two feet complete with a pair of wings.

One by one he counts the flying fowl, then he imprints their names, too, upon the child's memory.

Years change and centuries pass. The sandy island is in the middle of the atoll, lush and green amidst the blue of the ocean.

# Greedy

They tell of a time when the underwater world was calm and clear. The morning sun shone brightly.

At the end of a sandy beach bordered by a cliff, Andevavait, the amphibious tidepool blenny, was sunbathing. Beyond the water the fat-bellied toadfish, Bohurai, also known as Porobibi, reclined on a rock, where Andevavait lay in the sun. They were enjoying a chat. As he listened to Andevavait, Bohurai kept his eye on a fruit hanging from the shady trees above the water.

'I can't wait any longer,' Bohurai said to Andevavait. 'Friend, I can hardly follow our conversation, I'm so distracted by that fruit hanging up there.'

Andevavait looked around and said, 'What do you mean?'

'Try looking up!'

Pretending not to understand, Andevavait waggled his fin in the direction of the tree. 'That one up there?'

'Why, don't you know it?'

'Here we call it *anggadi*,' said Andevavait.

'Can you eat it?'

'Yes, of course you can eat it!'

'*Wah*, that big fruit?'

'You don't eat the whole thing.'

'What part of it do you eat?'

'The insides. It's delicious, but the skin is very hard …'

There was no further comment from Bohurai of the fat

belly. He was disappearing back into the coral as if he had been offended. Andevavait tried to call him back, but Bohurai was already upset, and Andevavait felt like he was talking to himself. Andevavait had no choice but to follow him.

'Dear friend,' said Andevavait, 'please come back. I'll tell you the secret of the coconut tree.'

Bohurai ignored him.

'I'm going to prove that I wasn't teasing you,' said the blenny.

Suddenly Andevavait disappeared from the surface of the water. A moment later a voice came from high above.

'Hey, Bohurai, come on up.'

Hearing his friend calling him from above, Bohurai wanted to climb up too. He was amazed to see Andevavait way up there, floating at the end of a coconut frond. Suddenly, Andevavait plunged towards him. Water splashed everywhere and the surface of the water was covered in ripples. Bohurai's fat body was flung about by the impact. The circular ripples went all the way to the shore and ended up on the sand. Andevavait was very happy to see his friend rocked by the disturbance but obviously impressed.

'Andev, you're a champion,' Bohurai said, once the water had calmed. 'But what was that thing you brought down with you?'

'A coconut! That's what you just asked me for.'

'You're trying to trick me again.'

'It's like this, my friend. There are certain conditions if you want to know the secrets of the coconut.'

'I'm not interested in the secrets,' said Bohurai. 'Just the coconut fruit. I want to try it.'

'Oh, I see. Are you really serious?'

'I'm serious. But don't go to a lot of trouble.'

'It's no trouble. Listen, my friend. First condition: you must learn to hold your breath.'

'And then?'

'The second condition is that you have to learn to put up with a hungry stomach.'

'That's easy! Is that all?' said Bohurai.

'Yes. To eat a coconut, my friend, first you must be able to hold your breath and put up with hunger.'

'Fine, if that's all, teach me to hold my breath!'

Bohurai started right away on his first lessons, from floating on the surface of the water to sunbathing under the sun, just as Andevavait did. Eventually, fat-belly Bohurai passed his breath-holding test. But Andevavait seemed to be in no hurry to bring down a coconut for him.

Bohurai wondered if his friend had been teasing him all along. But he began to be patient and followed Andevavait's advice. Now that he could hold his breath, he could see interesting things above the surface of the water and enjoy the beauty of a world that, until then, he knew could be visited by only a handful of sea creatures. By holding his breath, he could watch the animals that lived above the water, and appreciate all the compelling beauty of nature.

Now he could watch the changes that took place in nature from the moment the sun came up until it set. The instant it appeared, its gleaming light illuminated all the above-water creatures of the earth. At moments like that, he understood what was happening in his world beneath the sea. Bohurai had thought that this single source of light was close to the world, hovering just above the water. Now he realized that it was far away and unattainable. At last the toadfish understood why, every morning when the sun was about to rise, Andevavait disappeared up above water level.

He also saw the birds in the trees and heard their song. There were fowl that flew freely in the sky. There were creatures like him, who crept over the land. There were creatures that stood, propped up by two legs. And there were others with four legs.

'Andev, I really want to try that coconut. You can help me, can't you?' the toadfish begged him again.

'Of course I can,' said Andevavait, 'but can you fulfil the second condition, my friend? Because this is about controlling personal desire.'

'What sort of personal desire?'

'The kind that is never satisfied!'

'What do you mean? Give me an example.'

'You know, my friend, I usually adore eating those little prawns,' said Andevavait. 'I can't eat more than a dozen before I feel full. Now, what if I never felt satisfied and kept eating till I could hardly breathe? That's what I mean by controlling personal desire.'

'Oh, that's what's called being greedy!'

'So you already know what I'm talking about.'

'But what does that have to do with the coconut?'

'Some coconut palms grow on their own, but others are planted by people. We need to be aware of that. If the person that planted them is present, then it's not possible to take their fruit.'

'Oh, right. I thought they all grew wild, like things do under the sea: they belong to everyone. Whoever is quickest gets them.'

'My friend, the world above the water is different. Like the people who live in the villages here: they have their own customs. If they meet another person who wants to take a coconut because he's hungry, then that is allowed. The owner might even climb up to get the coconut himself and present it to his guest. When you want to pick coconuts and the owner isn't present, however, it's important not to take too many and not to forget to say thanks by leaving the coconut shell behind, under the tree. That way, when the owner shows up he won't worry. He'll think it was a friend or relative that left the coconut shell lying on the ground, because only family or friends are allowed to guard the village gardens.'

'Oh, in that case I'll leave it up to you,' said the toadfish.

'Good. You wait here and keep an eye out, and if any villagers show up give me a signal. Watch your head.'

Soon coconuts could be heard falling into the water.

'Is that enough?' Andevavait shouted down from the treetop. 'Or not yet?'

'Not yet, keep going, throw more down! Keep going!'

A bit later: 'Is that enough or not?'

'Not enough!'

'Hey, how many is enough?' Andevavait peeped down through the gaps in the coconut palm fronds.

'It's best you throw down some more. Later, I'll add them up and let you know if it's enough!'

'How many coconuts are down there?' shouted Andevavait.

'Andev, they've all drifted away!'

'Drifted away? How could that happen?'

'Just throw some more down, there's still plenty up there.'

'My friend, I'm exhausted. I'll throw down three more, and that's it!'

'Fine,' said Bohurai. 'Three is enough.'

Andevavait threw down three more coconuts, and with his last remaining strength climbed down the coconut palm. As he crawled down, he tried to remember exactly what had happened. With his friend's encouragement, he'd thrown down two entire bunches of coconuts. So how did Bohurai manage to save only a couple? When he reached the bottom of the tree, Andevavait leaned back on the trunk of the coconut palm exhausted.

Meanwhile, under the shade of the coconut tree, Bohurai the fat-belly was still lying in the water. His eyes felt heavy, and in his two fins he grasped two dry coconuts.

Andevavait was too tired to move. He watched Bohurai, and hoped that the bunch of young coconuts had already sunk to the bottom and were stuck in the coral. But where had the other lot, from the bunch of dry coconuts, drifted off to?

Someone else was also watching Bohurai: the striped crab, Anggereai. He crawled along the side of the rocks and suddenly scratched Bohurai's ear. The dozing fat-belly was taken by surprise. Stammering, he called out: 'An... Andevavait, we need one more coconut, then you can come down!'

Sliding up behind his friend, Andevavait said with a grin, 'Are you talking to me?'

Bohurai was astonished to find Andevavait right next to him.

'*Wah*,' said Bohurai. 'There are only two dry coconuts here. We need one more.'

'I'm exhausted,' Andevavait replied. 'You can have both those coconuts yourself.'

He was amazed at Bohurai's attitude. Like he'd done nothing wrong. And he was so quick to forget someone else's hard work. It looked like the crab, Anggereai, was also waiting for Bohurai to explain himself, but Bohurai ignored him and started to snore.

# The Tragedy

It was hot that morning and Andevavait, the tidepool blenny, had confined himself to a hole in the rock. He was fasting. He tried to go on a fast every low-tide season. It was his normal routine. While fasting, he was careful to keep away from his seawater world. Although he could hold his breath for hours out of the water, Andevavait always had to watch out for enemies. Predators lurked both under the water and above. There were barracuda and a gang of flat-tailed longtoms that liked to chase and prey on little fish like him. Both of these predators often visited this beach and the tip of its peninsula, because that was where the Endracht hardyhead and bareback anchovy lived and bred. Tawaiseng, the hookjaw moray eel, with his set of sharp teeth, also liked to hang out there. His head would appear from a hole in the reef and he would wait for an opportunity to attack his prey as they passed by. Because of his soft body, Andevavait the tidepool blenny was one of Tawaiseng's most favoured quarries.

That afternoon the tide was so low the whole coastline was dry. The reef where the fish normally hid was sticking way up out of the water. While fasting in his secret hole, Andevavait heard a groaning sound from the coral nearby. He thought he recognized the voice. Curiosity induced him to peep out at his surroundings. He worried that it might be a predator or kids from the village that could spot him, roll over the rock he was hiding under and capture him. If the grown-up people saw him, they would leave

Andevavait alone in his hiding place; they considered blennies too small to be worth hunting. But the kids thought capturing Andevavait and his kin a test of their dexterity. He was also afraid of predators on the land such as the monitor lizards or mice. And he could not ignore the threat of Kaintani, the kingfisher, or Awaingge, the beach heron.

After confirming that it was safe to venture out, Andevavait happily checked around the rocks to see if he could determine the source of the groaning in the coral wall. It turned out that the voice was that of Raukahi, an injured octopus.

'What's wrong, my friend?' Andevavait asked.

Raukahi showed him a fresh wound on the stump of one of his tentacles. 'I was swimming, searching for food, when suddenly Tawaiseng, the hookjaw moray, appeared and bit off one of my tentacles.' Now he only had seven tentacles left.

'Why didn't you just hide in your hole and wait for passing prey?' said Andevavait.

'Ah,' said the octopus. 'My hiding hole at the bottom of the ocean has been blown up by dynamite.'

It was lucky the octopus didn't have a bone structure like the fish, whose bones had been cracked by the explosion. The octopus had survived, but the fish world around him had been plunged into terrible grief and mayhem. Raukahi went on to describe the horror.

The fish that were near the blast had died immediately, their backbones instantly shattered. A cloud of sand and reef debris mixed with mud and sulphurous smoke had risen up and was carried by the current – then slowly a pile of dead fish could be seen settling at the bottom of the ocean. The fish that were a bit further away from the centre of the explosion also suffered fractured backbones; all they could do was swim in circles on the water's surface. The current dragged the dying fish until they finally expired and sank to the bottom. The radius of the pile of carcasses spread even wider. A few days later the surface of the water was covered in dead fish that had risen from the seabed. On the seashore, all along the waves' breaking point, the normal salty and delicious smell of the froth was now replaced by the stench of rotting fish.

After the trauma of the dynamite explosion that had almost killed him, the octopus didn't feel like taking advantage of the free food, even with thousands of dead and dying fish right there in front of him. He could only watch the feeding frenzy of the other predators: Paimani, the stingray, Tarubain, the highfin grouper, and even the *mandohai* sharks. He saw all the many members of the crab family out there, including Awein, the green lobster, who, along with his crab friends, preferred to pick out the fishes' eyes before eating their flesh.

Now Raukahi was homeless, without a hiding place. For the time being, he could dodge the ocean predators. But when the tide came in, he would have to quickly find a safer place.

# Andevavait's Sacrifice

It so happened that Andawai, a red-lined triggerfish, who had also become stuck in the reef because of the low tide, overheard the conversation between Andevavait the tidepool blenny and Raukahi the octopus. Mr Thick-skin Andevavait was sitting tight and fasting in his hole, not far from where the octopus was hiding. Andawai, who had a set of steel-strong teeth, had often been caught between tides, so he had become used to it and could hang around for ages in dry places.

'Poor Raukahi,' said Andawai. 'I'm sorry to see what's happened to you. If you like, we can get together at the turn of the tide and I can help you find a new home.'

'Maybe ... I don't know.' Raukahi was still paranoid and couldn't be sure whether if he could trust Andawai.

Andevavait, who understood Andawai's good intentions, soon addressed the octopus's concerns.

'My friend, Raukahi, you're still young, right?' Andevavait tried to guess Raukahi's age.

'Yes, but why are you concerned about my age?'

'Why? Because if you were experienced, Raukahi, you would not lose a tentacle.'

'You think I'm inexperienced?'

'Unless, of course, you lost your tentacle because you let it happen.'

'*Wah*, would I let it happen?'

As far back as Raukahi remembered, ever since humans had caught his mother, he had been fighting to survive. He had protected his hole, where his family lived, from wild octopus. Now he lived alone. He had experienced all kinds of adventures under the sea: preying on a number of sea creatures, to changes of shape and skin colour, right up the tragedy of the dynamite explosion. Now, tiny Andevavait – this little blenny fish who lived only in the shallows, too afraid to dive into deeper waters – was calling him inexperienced!

'Oh! Ouch, it hurts!' Raukahi screamed and licked the stump of his tentacle.

'Oh dear ... that wound will have to be treated as soon as possible,' said Andevavait.

'What should I do?'

'My friend, you have to treat that wound before the high tide arrives. If you wait too long you will tempt more danger.'

'Don't try to scare me!'

'I'm not making it up. And you should be scared. Saliva won't be enough to get rid of the fishy smell. The odour will draw predators that like the fishy smell or the scent of blood.'

'Please help me!' said the octopus.

'My friend, keep calm. Keep licking your wound, but be careful that you don't use up all your saliva.'

Andevavait was already pondering how he could get far enough inland to pick a mixture of medicinal herbs before the tide came in. For him, this was not just a personal challenge – it could also be a life and death gamble. He would have to cross the small channel with chunks of coral reef leading toward the sand, all the while keeping an eye out for his predators from the land. The one he feared most was Kaintani, the kingfisher. This bird, a hunter of beach crabs, had attacked Andevavait once before. It was lucky for Andevavait he had only just emerged from the water, because when the kingfisher's claws grabbed him his body was still wet and slippery. He managed to wriggle free and fell back into the water.

Before crossing, Andevavait peeked out from behind the rock and looked up at the branch of the *bitau* tree where the kingfisher liked to perch. The most shady *bitau* branch looked empty. But Andevavait tried to be patient. He was right to hesitate, because when his eyes scanned the beach he saw Kaintani catch a crab. If he moved now and the kingfisher noticed him, he would definitely be able to get away, because even if the kingfisher noticed him, his beak would still be full of crab. If he started to cross right away, the kingfisher would have just swallowed his prey, and would be flying back to his perch.

The challenge would arise after he had managed to get the medicinal plants and was on his way back across the sand and the ditch. From his open perch, Kaintani could easily glide over and catch him. He'd be lucky if Kaintani's stomach was already full – you could tell if he was full if he started to clean his beak and chest feathers with one of his wings. Then he would fly to the forest and disappear.

But what if the bird's stomach wasn't full yet? If Andevavait didn't act soon, the tide would come in and it would be a disaster for the octopus. If he moved right away, he would risk his own life. Andevavait peeped out again. He was right, Kaintani was back on his normal perch. His chest was white, with a vest of royal blue that matched his wings. His eyes were clear black, watchful, and able to pierce every eye and heart that they saw. Andevavait was nervous; perhaps he should give up. Unable to take the risk, there was nothing he could do but wait, as the octopus became more and more agitated with his wound.

'Andevavait, are you seriously trying to help?' said Raukahi.

'Relax, friend. I'll soon get the medicine for your wound.'

'Please hurry. Why haven't you left yet? The tide is coming in and soon this place will fill up with water.'

'Just be patient, friend. It's not yet safe out there.'

At the furthest tip of the promontory, two people could be seen paddling their single outrigger canoe towards the beach. Andevavait had to make use of this opportunity. While keeping an eye on Kaintani, he also watched the canoe approaching. The kingfisher was getting restless, his sight was no longer focused on the beach, but shifted to the canoe that would soon pass the *bitau* tree. Andevavait was right: as soon as the canoe approached, Kaintani, the kingfisher, flew away. At that moment Andevavait took off as fast as he could, before the canoe could reach the beach.

When the man and his wife paddled their canoe close the shore, the man exploded with rage, shouting as he looked for something under the coconut tree. The wife sounded angry too – she was cursing. And what was the cause of all their anger? They were both furious about the coconuts that had disappeared from the top of their palm tree.

# A Bamboo-cutting Ritual

Andevavait was trapped. The canoe and the angry husband and wife were blocking his path back to the octopus's hiding place. He desperately sought a way out. How could he get there quickly, before the high tide filled up Raukahi's secret hiding place? Once more Andevavait had to wait. He hoped the village couple would leave soon. While he racked his brain to find a solution, Andevavait chewed on *nanna*, wild coriander leaves, to make a healing medicine for his friend's wounds.

Oh no!

All of a sudden Andevavait noticed the village woman was walking back towards the ocean and across the ditch. She was turning over the rocks that stuck out above the low tide.

Oh no, this will be the end of the octopus, thought Andevavait.

And next up would of course be his little red-striped friend, Andawai, who was under the neighbouring stone. While the woman continued picking up bits of coral and grabbing shells or fish that were trapped behind the stones, her husband headed into the forest beside the promontory, carrying a machete.

This was Andevavait's best chance, to follow the flow of the small river along the length of the slope, ignoring all the dangers of the fresh water. Then the man appeared again. He crossed the river and approached the estuary, dragging with him a few fine *fayamai* bamboo branches.

My goodness, that man with the brown, sunburned face is

getting angrier and all because of the missing coconuts, thought Andevavait. The man's breathing was now audible, and becoming faster and faster. Andevavait could hear him gasping for breath.

Andevavait had already entered the river, but now there was a pile of bamboo right in front of his face. There was no way he could stop. The thrust of the current pushing him towards the beach was strong. If he jumped out of the water he would get stuck on the bamboo branches. If he leapt up to the surface he would be caught up in the bamboo twigs. If he went any deeper he couldn't be sure that he would be able to get back to the surface safely. Besides, he was not used to diving in fresh water. His decision to swim and glide across the fresh water now seemed reckless. He had taken the risk to save his friend's life. But if he decided to take another risk and dive even deeper he might run into Amaren, the freshwater eel, or Anotar, the snakehead. He might even be caught by Aifa, the karaka crab.

Andevavait gave up, allowing his body to be dragged by the current, and he crashed into the bamboo twigs. All he could do was to close his eyes, keeping his mouth shut as tight as he possible so the chewed-up leaves wouldn't escape and disappear in the current. For a moment he was caught between the branches and dragged towards the beach. Luckily he was able to free himself and roll onto the sand.

Andevavait's body floundered. Shaking off the sand, he flopped all the way to the edge of the river mouth and then leapt back towards the water. Diving quickly under the water so the woman wouldn't see him, he finally reached his friend's hiding place. But the rock had moved and it was upside down. The water around it was cloudy, and he couldn't make out the hole where the octopus had hidden.

As he moved through the murky water, Andevavait bumped into the lower part of the woman's leg. She got a big fright and instinctively jumped away. Bending over, she looked around to see what kind of sea creature had surprised her. But Andevavait had already slipped over the stones and was keeping an eye on the woman's movement. Even though the rock he was seeking had been moved, he was hoping that the poor octopus would still be there. The question was, had he survived or had he been thrown into the woman's basket?

The woman took a step back, then turned around and headed towards her husband, her steps parting the water. The tide was already high, right up to her knees. As soon as she reached the shore, she started walking faster toward the man.

Then she realized what her husband was doing.

She stopped. She turned away and moved slowly back towards the ocean. It looked as if she was talking to herself. Her face had the pained expression of a supplicant begging for mercy. Perhaps she was voicing her worries to the ocean, maybe to her ancestors – to those departed souls who visited often enough. They stayed around her grandmother. She could feel their presence, and whenever they showed up, her grandmother was happy.

'*Imariraoo* …!' she wailed.

Her shoulder basket and *noken*, the bag she wore slung across her forehead, came loose and fell to the ground. The woman's body seemed to have suddenly become boneless, and crumpled between the basket and the *noken*. Her cries rang out as she wailed through her tears.

'I don't want it! I don't want to have to suffer again. I don't want my womb to become a victim, my children victims. I don't want it. I don't want people talking behind my back. People saying that my womb is a place for the dead. I repent; I am beaten. I repent; I am kicked! *Imariraoo* …!'

Whatever the husband was doing at that moment had obviously terrified her. But there was no way she could stop him from carrying out the bamboo-cutting ritual. There he was, swearing upon the spirits of their ancestors, asking for a blessing from the great Creator of the sky and the earth on which all mankind stands. As he chanted the curse, he slashed away at the broken piece of bamboo. This ritual could have deadly consequences; it would doubtless end in someone's death. Someone unknown to the curser might die, or someone who had done them wrong. But the chances were that the results of the ritual would rebound upon the very person who carried it out.

Perhaps the ritual required some kind of premature mourning, to deflect its most probable consequences, which the woman had already suffered, time and time again.

'Just this once,' she begged, 'could the curse please move elsewhere, be passed on to somebody else's family?'

Her husband looked grim as he pushed bamboo stakes into the ground. He planted them at cross-angles just below the stepped roots at the base of the coconut palm. This was a sign that it was now forbidden to climb the tree. No exception would be granted. Not even his wife or children could climb it. When he heard her protesting, he was almost distracted from carrying out the ritual. But if he stopped now because of her, he knew that she would be the one to reap the disaster, so he carried on.

Once the ritual was complete, the man appeared more relaxed and he approached his wife. With a single movement he jerked her up onto her feet, but she collapsed back to the sand. Her husband dragged her along the beach, ignoring her basket and *noken* head-bag that had been left behind. The woman was hauled along sobbing. When he arrived at his canoe he slipped his machete into the boat and then roughly picked up and tossed the woman after it.

Treated in this way, as if she were a useless piece of meat, his wife could only remain silent and resign herself to the outcome. When the canoe was finally back on the water, her husband did not start paddling immediately; he remained for a while floating under the coconut tree, staring up at the fruit still left on the palm. After a short pause he began slowly paddling his canoe, still looking back at the beach. Finally he gave voice, shouting to all who could hear.

'Hey! Tomorrow! Maybe in the morning or in the afternoon – we will come back. We will come and get our coconuts from the trees that were planted by our ancestors. All of us, together; we will feast upon them and they will give our bodies strength!'

# Contemplating Fate

It was almost noon when the high tide and the sea breeze arrived, both at the same time. Andevavait was still staring blankly from the top of a rock. He looked stunned, as if he had just realized that he had experienced something amazing. In fact he had almost been killed. Now, the tide was already high and it was too late for him to help Raukahi the octopus. He imagined what it would be like when the water cleared and the underwater life that had stopped because of the low tide, was once again revived. Then this area would once more become a hunting ground, crowded with visitors from the deep sea. As was usual when the tide went out, the larger fish that lived in this habitat had moved out to deeper parts. Way out there, they would try to ignore their hunger until the tide came back in and filled up the bay.

This was a time when tips of seaweed, small fish and other living things could die, trapped in the dry patches or burnt by the rays of the sun. The fishy aroma of dead marine life signalled a routine feast for those who had fled and withstood their hunger – especially for the fish in this area. The roots of the coral and seaweed that had been pulled out or snapped off because of the bad mood of that village woman added to the fishy aroma, and that meant that predators would soon arrive for a feast.

And in one of those dangerous spots was Raukahi the octopus, nursing his fresh wound. Andevavait imagined that the octopus's flesh, so tender and succulent, would be a special treat for predators.

Andevavait began to feel a stinging sensation on the part of his skin that had been soaking in the water, so he moved to a dryer part of the rock. He saw that his skin was scraped. He regretted his recklessness in helping the octopus. He had almost sacrificed his own life. Now he couldn't help anymore. He realized that he must heal his own wounds before taking any more risks. Meanwhile, he should stay in the safest possible place, on top of the bit of rock that stuck out of the water.

Smearing his wound with some of the chewed-up *nanna* leaves that he had intended for the octopus, Andevavait focused his mind on finding a new place. That infernal woman had destroyed his resting place, his fasting spot and his food store.

For the moment he decided to stay put. The most important thing was that he was in a safe spot. He continued to treat his wounds where the skin was scraped. It must have happened when he was trapped in the bamboo branches and dragged along in the sand. He should have been more patient and waited until the couple from the village had gone. Even so, he still couldn't help the octopus. But now that the couple had left, would it be safe for him to go back? It was the presence of that pair of humans that had driven away the usual predators that dominated the place, and prevented them from coming back.

Instinctively he remembered the threat of Kaintani the kingfisher, and Andevavait's eyes moved back to the *bitau* tree. The shady branches of the tree were still empty, but Andevavait realized that he was very exposed in this wide-open place. The only way he could save himself was by jumping into the water.

But he wouldn't be able to withstand the pain of the cuts where his skin had been scraped off. And, most dangerous of all, his wounds would soon release a fishy odour.

It was in this state of mind – feeling anxious and overwhelmed – that Andevavait suddenly saw a sombre shadow flash over the water's surface and swoop past his head. Instantly, Andevavait leapt into the water. A moment later he was back on the surface. The source of the shadow was Kafoni, a red eagle that had just swooped down on his prey, not far from Andevavait.

Goodness, thought Andevavait, if it had been me caught in that deadly clench, that would have been the end of my life's story.

Andevavait quickly checked to see whether the remaining concoction of medicine on his wound had mixed with the salt water. Luckily, the medicinal paste was still there. At the very least there was enough to treat his wounds for a few days. Now he must find a new place to hide so he could safely recuperate.

He felt very sorry for the other small fish like himself. They had to be careful at all times if they wanted to enjoy the beauty of this life for long. If he compared the fate of the *ainai*, the hard-headed fishes that usually gathered in large schools, with his own, Andevavait was still better off. In spite of his body being as small as a human's middle finger, Andevavait lived alongside small gatherings of his fellow species, their dwellings spread out all along the rocky seashore. In the quieter areas of the beach that were less frequently visited by humans, a crowd of Andevavait's fellows could sometimes be seen when the water drained back out after the waves had crashed onto the rocks. They liked to stay in close touch with each other.

But in an area sometimes visited by people, such as Andevavait's habitat in this story, there were only a few of his kind left, at the most less than a dozen. So why then, did Andevavait live alone? It seemed to be his fate to live a lonely life. And now his house had been turned upside down. He decided to stay on in an open place until his wounds recovered.

Then surely he could dive in and look for the entrance to his house. But even if he could dive again and find his hidey-hole, he would have to be very careful and first observe it from a distance, to make sure that no other living creatures had taken over the house. If it happened to be Moa, a ferocious eel that had moved in, then he would have to give it up for his own safety.

That place used to belong to Aidorehi, a mangrove worm. But ever since the black ash plague exploded in the environs of this beach, every worm in his tribe had died, including Aidorehi and his family. Aidorehi's house had been left empty, so Andevavait had decided to take it over.

Now the tide was up to its highest point and the wind was blowing stronger; even the clarity of the seawater had improved. Although the water's surface was rippled, from on top of his stone Andevavait could still plainly see the activities taking place under the water. He could see that there were more fish visiting than usual, scavenging amongst the soft algae sticking to the rocks. How appetizing it was to see the remaining seaweed roots and rock moss being swarmed over by all the different species of fish.

He knew that the *amumar* or moon wrasse would always be more active than others in leading the group of algae-eaters.

These flirtatious and sprightly fly fish went round and round fiddling with anything they suspected might be edible. The results of an *amumar* investigation would instantly get a response from the others. Andevavait knew most of the scavenger fish in this area and was familiar with their ways. Especially the *amumar* – they were so lively and active, but they had no principles at all. This green fish with its military camouflage and black spots, was forever changing its mind, and was Mr Fickle himself.

# The Village Under the Moon

Just across from the land was a hill that stuck up in the middle of an island. Surrounding the island was a chain of small atolls. On the hill was a village, and at the foot of the hill a spring that provided the source of life for all the inhabitants.

The one who had discovered it said that the spring had appeared at the place where a firebird had fallen from the sky. They call it 'the village under the moon', because it was said that the moon came down to sit upon the village rooftops at every full moon, appearing to be drifting as if in a dream. Resting there, the moon was said to meditate silently, giving out a flickering light that seemed to be spread by fireflies and reflected endlessly in the glowing ocean.

The golden gleam....
shimmering pearl,
decorating mist
drifting, flowing, seeping
into the sago leaf roofs,
interspersed with tin.
Conversing in the billowing breath of the hearth
warming the rise of the morning star,
leaving coals in leaden darkness.
A sublime fragrance creeps over the earth
as the moon rolls up its mat, so high above the village,
washing its face in view of the sun.

In the night, when the sky is bright and sprinkled with stars, the men of the village would gather and share the stories from their day – stories of hunting near the village or gardening or fishing in the ocean.

When fishing in the ocean, there are a number of ways for men to fish as a group, and each method serves to strengthen the emotional bonds of that group.

The Mangga-erang people, for example, are a group of fisherman that use nets. A number of outriggers set out together on a fishing expedition. This is a time for members of the younger generation to tag along and learn about the many different types of fish.

On board the canoes, the young ask their elders about the fish they are unfamiliar with, and they learn about the system of sharing the day's catch, a method gleaned from experience.

The entire harvest of the Mangga-erang fishing people is put together and then shared equally. The front-man, who sits at the bow of the canoe, the helmsman in the stern and the one who sits in the middle all get an equal share, and they don't forget to keep some for the owners of the nets and the canoes as well.

The Mangga-maraing people, on the other hand, are a group of line fishermen. They practice tug fishing, jigging, and bottom fishing. Their fishing parties are smaller, generally just two or three people in one canoe, or one person in his own boat.

Unlike the Mangga-erang, they don't pool their catch with others. Every boat gets to keep its own full catch, sharing only with the owner of the outrigger. If there are three people in one boat, then the catch will be divided into four. If there are two people in one canoe then the catch is divided into three. Even if one fisherman goes fishing in his own boat, the catch is still divided. With whom you might ask? Only that man and his wife would know the answer. If the Mangga-maraing man is alone, and not yet married and has an over-flowing catch, it will be even harder to guess. No doubt in his mind he will already have a list of plans, in the shape of money or goods that he may purchase. Apart from his personal consumption, all that has been put aside in the canoe remains right there, in between the outriggers.

And in reality, on his journey home, these plans are likely to change at any moment. When passing a boat returning from the fields, for example, carrying husband, wife and child, they greet each other. Sometimes the farmer, paddling his way home from the fields will make a joke, calling out: 'Hey Mangga-maraing, what kind of rocks did you lift out of the ocean? Your boat looks as if it's sinking!'

With pleasure the fisherman will respond: 'That is true – because of these rocks I have become tired and sleepy. It seems as if I can see smoke coming from the fields. Maybe that smoke will banish my tiredness.'

The boats pull up alongside each other. Cigarettes, referred to by the fisherman as 'smoke', are offered around. While the cigarettes are lit and smoke billows around the face of the fisherman, amazement will be seen upon the faces from the fields, as they view the day's catch piled up inside the canoe.

The young man of the Mangga-maraing will then share the catch in his canoe with the group on their way back from the fields. The people from the fields would try their hardest to stop him throwing fish in their canoe, because the Mangga-maraing man will only consider that the share is equal if the word 'Enough!' has been said many times. Equality in this case is not measured by one cigarette, but rather because a big catch of fish should always be shared equally with others.

In return, part of the harvest from the field would then be loaded into the Mangga-maraing canoe. The break-even point would only be achieved, once more, when the young man has protested: 'Enough! Enough ...' and 'Enough!' again. As a thank-you bonus, the fisherman will then throw a few extra fish into the farmer's canoe.

It is a no-win situation, however, when the boats that get together are from the village of coconuts known as 'Sleepy Village' because those canoes are sure to carry *je anggadi* coconut palm wine or *je vereng*, the 'sleepy drink' made from the *nipah* palm. Smoke will then billow from the joined canoes, and it will be up to the wind to decide where the two boats drift. And meanwhile, what about the original course of heading home to the village? That will surely be forgotten for quite some time.

The Mangga-Jee is group of fishermen who hunt their prey using absolutely nothing. The male children gather on their canoes, but only to listen. There they learn about human nature and characteristics that are described in a similar way to those of fish and other animals. If there is an adult or child present who behaves like a particular fish, then he will be given that fish's name as his nickname. Sometimes the nickname lasts only for a moment, but sometimes it lasts all his life and becomes a story told by his grandchildren.

# The Risks of Hunting

The sound of a wild dog barking beside the stream woke Andevavait the tidepool blenny from his daydreams. The wild dog kept barking as he ran along the bank of the river, following the flow of the water until it reached the point where the river met the sea, and there he stopped.

This skinny, mangy dog was looking for something. He raised his snout in the air, as if sensing the direction of the wind with his nostrils. Then he turned and ran back the way he had come, stopping now and then to sniff at his paw prints.

He eventually turned towards the place where the woman from the village had collapsed earlier and had then been dragged away by her husband. There, Skinny the mangy dog found a bag that consisted of woven palm leaves, kisses, sniffs and sneezes, all of which he would shortly abandon as he headed off in yet another direction.

Andevavait was watching the movements of Skinny – the dog already had his nose inside the basket, and what would he find there? Andevavait's body stiffened, both his fins felt as if they were standing up on end alongside his head, and his eyes were wide open in anticipation.

Suddenly the dog yelped in pain, jumping around and shaking his head. This dance was caused by a crab. It was Aiweirori the flower crab, with his long pincers. He had clamped onto Skinny's lip and he didn't want to let go.

In a flash the body of the stripy blue crab was thrown far away, landing at the water's edge. There the crab's body remained, spread-eagled and motionless except for the froth bubbling from its mouth. Although his body had been cast off and was now dead, his claw seemed to have found a new partner, and there it remained, hanging tightly to the lip of the wild dog.

What absolute bad luck! The dog kept yelping. In a panic he ran, he buried his face in the sand, he rolled around and rubbed the tip of his nose. It didn't work. Finally he got up and ran into the forest, his lip's new soul mate still clinging fast. The yelping and sobbing cries finally disappeared, swallowed up by the forest's silence.

Andevavait took a deep breath and his fins went slack, allowing him to lie back on the rocks. He was torn by mixed emotions – of sadness at the tragedy that had befallen the crab, Aiweirori, and amusement at the bad luck of the wild dog from the forest. He scanned the beach up and down, but Aiweirori's body had disappeared, already washed away by the waves.

Now he was reminded of the activities of Amumar, the moon wrasse, and his friends, but the water around that area had turned black. Amumar and the gang of scavengers had gone, he didn't know where. Andevavait knew that the culprit must be a squid. Or could it have been the wounded octopus?

Andevavait had a good look around and then finally he found his answer. There was Raukahi the octopus, on the outer side of the rock. With half his body still immersed in the water, he held his wounded tentacle up in the dry air. At least his friend was still alive. Andevavait quickly moved next to the octopus. His friend was still gasping.

'Raukahi, where have you been, my friend? I've been so worried!'

'*Wah*, that was almost it …' said Raukahi, trying to calm his breathing.

'Almost it? Almost what?' Feeling sorry for the octopus, Andevavait said, 'Come up on the rock before the water becomes too clear.'

'Thanks, but it's all right. You can let me be as long as my wounded tentacle remains safe in a dry place.'

'Yes, but Amumar and his friends will be back soon.'

'What's that about Amumar?'

'You don't know about that scavenger?'

'I don't know!'

'That Amumar is naughty, like Kowar, the Whitley's sergeant fish. They are both cheeky and love stirring up trouble.'

'If I make myself the same colour as the rock, would they recognize me?'

'That Amumar's just like a fly, he approaches anything that looks suspicious, especially if that something has an inviting scent. Remember, my friend, your wound hasn't been treated yet.'

Andevavait inspected the octopus's wound and brought out the rest of the herbal medicine that he had tucked away behind his cheek.

Seeing his wound was about to be treated, the octopus moved up onto the rock.

'That's the way! Now, tell me what happened. You almost … what?' asked Andevavait as he doctored Raukahi's wound.

'I can't talk about it!'

'Why not?' said Andevavait.

Raukahi said nothing, but his body suddenly started trembling.

Andevavait felt the sudden change in him, and he quickly finished treating his wound. 'Does your wound hurt?' He was worried that the *nanna* leaf concoction he had made was causing the octopus to tremble.

But the octopus just shook his head and answered weakly, 'No, I'm just traumatized and scared, thinking about the dreadful thing that just happened.'

Andevavait tried to soothe the octopus. 'My dear friend, first of all you must relax.'

'Thank you. The medicine feels cool on my wound.'

'You're welcome. My friend, I almost got caught, too. On my way back I got tangled in some bamboo branches. Luckily I escaped, although it cost me some skin. Fortunately I had your medicine with me, so I could use it to treat my own wounds.'

Andevavait showed his wounds to the octopus.

'I'm sorry. This is all my fault.'

'Never mind, it's in the past now,' said Andevavait. He tried to forget his ordeal.

Then Raukahi tilted his head a bit. 'Andev, would you check my neck? It hurts!'

Andevavait was horrified at what he saw: 'Oh, my friend, it looks like a snakebite. Or could it have been a different animal?'

'Indeed, today I have been extremely unlucky!'

'Tell me, friend, what kind of animal was it?'

'I don't know, some kind of devil suddenly pounced on me.'
'Devil? Where?'
'At the beach!'
'How did you end up in that dry place?'
'When you left to get the medicine, I waited. I was so worried, wondering if you could make it back or not.'

Raukahi stopped. By his face it seemed he was recalling something frightening.

'Tell me what happened!' said Andevavait.

'Imagine how you would feel if suddenly a person appears and starts rolling over stones and tearing the rocks apart. It was like an earthquake! I fought back with all my strength. It felt like the world was spinning upside down. I don't know what happened. When I came to, my head was already in the woman's grip. But then, the woman squeezed my mouth. I tried to bite her hand but I couldn't. Spontaneously my tentacles spread, sucking and coiling up to the top of her arm. The woman just let my tentacles creep all the way up to her neck and cheek. Then her left hand took something strange from the cavern of her mouth. She took out a lump of tobacco mixed with her saliva and stuffed it into my mouth. Instantly my vision was blurred and my energy flew away, completely gone! After that I don't remember a thing.'

'Oh no! My friend! And then what?'

'Well, when I woke up ...' Raukahi gasped. 'I discovered I had been lucky!'

'Why, what happened?'

Raukahi's thoughts drifted somewhere far away. Andevavait tried to guess what was going through the mind of his friend the octopus. After a few moments, he prompted Raukahi to continue his story. 'And when you woke up?'

'I was awake, but I couldn't do anything, because I was so weak and I was trapped in the basket.'

'Now I'm beginning to understand. There must have been another animal in that woman's basket!'

'So you saw?'

'Yes, I was watching the woman and her man when they arrived in the canoe.'

'Oh! And then …?'

'Why weren't you still under the rock?' scolded Andevavait.

'You know what it was like outside. When I came to, I couldn't see the woman. I didn't realize that her man was still there.'

Raukahi and Andevavait fell quiet. Lost deep in thought, they tried to connect the events that each had experienced.

Raukahi said, 'Andev, tell me what happened when you went to get the medicine.'

'Ah, my friend, keep telling me your story. I'll tell you mine later, after you have finished yours.'

'Ah, dear friend!' said Raukahi. 'When I came to, I felt like I was being stabbed by a knife. I opened my eyes slowly, and what did I see? The crab, Aiweirori, was walking over my body! If I screamed, it would hurt even more. So I focused on protecting my eyes and my wounded tentacle from the crab's feet.'

'So Aiweirori was still alive?' asked Andevavait.

'If he was dead how could he be walking all over me!'

'Was it just the two of you in the basket?'

'No! There was also Uneng, the yellow-lined sea perch!'

'At that time did you hear any other voices?'

Raukahi didn't respond. It seemed like he didn't want to go on. He moved to a more comfortable part of the rock. Then he checked the wound marks where the crab's feet had pierced his skin and the bite on his neck.

Andevavait waited for Raukahi to continue his story. But the octopus was settling into a comfortable resting position.

'You can't go to sleep now!' growled Andevavait. But the octopus still chose to keep his mouth shut. Andevavait tried to tempt Raukahi.

'My friend, I just saw a yellow fish being attacked by a *kafoni*, a red eagle. Has that got anything to do with Uneng, the yellow-lined sea perch that was in the basket with you?'

Andevavait's plan worked: it stirred the octopus to speak. 'That's why you should listen until it's finished when someone else is telling the story.'

'I'm sorry. I understand. Won't you go on?'

'Of course! Rather than letting my skin get worse, I gathered all my energy and climbed out of the basket. I was half out of the basket when Uneng, the perch, started to flop around. Aiweirori went on full alert. With both his arms stretched out, he took up half of the space in the basket. His back was tight against the wall of the basket. He seemed to get taller as he stretched up on tiptoe. Then Uneng flopped and breathed his last. His spine pierced one of my tentacles. The pain was unbearable and I screamed. Then Aiwei's claw grabbed Uneng. Crazy! He got my tentacle, too, which was still stuck to Uneng's back.'

Andevavait stared in fascination and his fins were stiff. When he realized that Raukahi had noticed, he relaxed his fins. But he could barely stay still and wait.

'That's amazing. Go on, my friend,' said Andevavait.

'The pain was so bad I peed. I was still weak. My wound still hurt and my tentacle was squeezed in Aiwei's claw. And I had been stabbed by Uneng's spine – my suffering was complete.' Raukahi took a breath.

'What about the bite wound in the back of your head?' said Andevavait. 'How did that happen?'

'Be patient, Andev, just listen! Where was I? Uneng died in Aiwei's clench along with my tentacle. Aiwei's fate wasn't so good either – he was badly wounded. There was a wound like a hole that went from Aiwei's back all the way through to his chest. But it just made him wilder and more angry.

'Trapped in that danger, I got a boost of energy and suddenly I pulled my whole body out of the basket, except for the tentacle that remained pinned to Uneng's body. If my energy had been more stable I would have responded to Aiwei's attack. With my tentacles, I could have coiled myself around Aiwei's body until he ran out of breath. I could even have crushed his shell, like I do when I prey on smaller crabs or shrimp.

'The other thing not in my favour was that I wasn't used to spending a lot of time out of the water like *andevavait* or *anggereai*. I had to get back into the water as quickly as possible; I desperately needed my natural habitat, my native country.'

Raukahi went on. 'I was desperate. I used all my remaining strength to pull. But it turned out I was holding on to sand, so it was useless. You can't get a grip on sand, not like a rock or a tree trunk. Aiwei tightened his clench even harder. I screamed as my bladder was being squeezed really hard. Both Aiwei's claws were squeezing Uneng's body.

'That's when I heard a growling sound behind me, and then I felt my neck being bitten. I didn't see anything, but suddenly my head was in a disgustingly smelly mouth. I fought with my tentacles, the bite was released, and – can you imagine? – I was flung high into the air and I fell down beside the river. At first I thought I was dead. But luckily I made it back here.'

'Now your story is starting to become clearer,' said Andevavait.

'Danger really can come from every direction,' said the octopus. 'But it's late in the afternoon now. Andev, are you feeling what I'm feeling?'

'Yes, I also feel like it's getting quite late in the afternoon,' Andevavait answered in a rather offhand way.

'That's not what I meant. I was just asking, do you feel what I feel?'

'Feel what, friend?' said Andevavait.

'I asked you, now you're asking me back?'

'Come on, what feeling do you have?'

'I'm hungry!' said Raukahi.

'*Wah*! Such a struggle just to say that!'

'Do you feel hungry or not?'

'I don't know. I'm still fasting. You should fast too. Especially with your wounds. Meanwhile, my friend, you mustn't go into the ocean and hunt for food.'

'Why does it have to be like that?' said the octopus, curling up to sleep.

Andevavait didn't know what he should do next. He had only just realized that, from that morning's low tide right up until the high tide in the afternoon, Anggereai the striped crab had still not appeared. This camouflage-green crab was Andevavait's best friend. He often called him Bayau the intelligence agent.

Anggereai the crab was the most loyal guard of the shallows and always recorded any changes that happened along the shoreline. If Andevavait was around, Anggereai was bound to be there as well. When the tide was high and the area undisturbed by humans, Anggereai would set off and explore the land or the steep cliff sides.

Sometimes when he was bored, the crab would climb a coconut tree and stay there for hours, just to daydream or snore. Even so, Anggereai was incredibly alert, and Andevavait depended on him greatly. If Andevavait wanted to climb a coconut tree, all he had to do was whistle to Anggereai, and the crab would reply with a signal telling him if the situation was safe or if there was a threat of danger.

'Where could Anggereai be?' said Andevavait to himself.

The last time he had seen Anggereai was when he was picking coconuts for Bohurai. He wanted to call him with a whistle, but the octopus was there: he might remember the whistle and their secret way of communicating. Andevavait glanced in the direction of the octopus. Raukahi still looked as if he was in a daydream and he gazed back blankly at Andevavait. Suddenly Andevavait slapped his forehead.

'Stupid. No wonder!' he said to himself.

Andevavait suddenly understood why his friend had

disappeared. The favourite prey of the octopus was the meat of crabs like Anggereai. Andevavait wondered how he could meet Anggereai and explain why the octopus happened to be there, albeit temporarily while he was undergoing treatment and learning to much.

Would Anggereai understand this or would he think that Andevavait had conspired with Raukahi to trap him? Or maybe Anggereai would think that Andevavait had told the octopus about their little secret. Andevavait was confused, and he started banging his head against the rock, and saying 'Stupid, stupid, stupid –'

'You're the stupid one,' said the fasting octopus, suddenly aroused from his stupor. 'Why are you calling me stupid?'

'What's the matter? I'm talking to myself, not to anyone else.'

'You're lying. You just said that I'm stupid and now you're pretending that you didn't.'

'You're being over-sensitive!' said Andevavait.

'Sensitive! You're angry because I haven't finished my story, right?'

'Mr Seven-fingers! Even if you didn't tell me, I was a witness to your sad story!'

'Then why do you keep asking me about it?' The octopus let his emotions run loose.

'I wanted to know who else was in that basket. Because if that's what happened, it means Andawai the red-lined triggerfish must have escaped from that woman as well.'

Andevavait instantly checked the water's surface, but the group of fish that normally clustered there was nowhere to be seen. Usually before the sun set, the scavenger fish would race in to fill up their bellies. Why was there no sign of those fish, normally led by Kowar or Amumar? Andevavait decided to quit his fasting and dive into the water to find out about the absence of the scavenger fish, including Andawai.

First he examined his wounds and found them all healed.

'My dear, I have to quit fasting and dive in right away to check on my other friends,' Andevavait said to Raukahi.

'Don't do that! You have to stay here until I have healed completely.'

'Yes, of course! But now my own wounds have healed, so I can dive into the water any time now.'

'Don't leave me here alone!' Raukahi begged.

'It's safe – I'll be right back.' Andevavait plunged into the water, but within a few moments he was back again, shaking off drops of water and wetting Raukahi, who already looked a bit panicky.

'My friend, I forgot to tell you, you have to wet your skin frequently so it will remain healthy. If you let it go dry, the fishy smell will become sharper, inviting little flying creatures to swarm your body. Even worse, when night comes, there will be an army of mosquitoes here.'

'Thanks, Andev, I don't feel the stinging of my wounds anymore.'

'Good. It means they are beginning to heal.'

'So I can soak in the water again?'

'You may, but don't stay in for too long, not until you have your own house where you will be sheltered from danger.'

'Thanks, Andev, and thank you for the medicine. When my fast is over, I'll be on my way.'

'Where will you go?' Andevavait asked.

'I don't know.'

'My friend, you stay here. I will look for Andawai to get him to fulfil his promise.'

'Promise?'

'You don't remember?'

'I do remember, but I just don't trust that thick-skinned Andawai,' said the octopus.

'My friend Andawai the triggerfish never lies.'

'Can you guarantee that?'

'It's like this, my friend. Andawai is a very superior fish. As a sea creature, he has passed the fasting test and he understands the world above the water quite well. Andawai always pulls his weight as a hard worker, and if he makes a promise he will hold it forever.'

'Just looking at him makes me nervous,' said Raukahi.

'For now, my friend, you should wait here while you adjust your camouflage to the changes around you. I will look for Andawai right away and at the same time check on Anggereai the crab. I'm worried about why it's so quiet out there. Maybe a predator has entered the area.'

This time Andevavait was a lot more cautious. Sinking his head back into the water, he carefully checked out the situation under the sea.

# Initiation and Karma

It was late in the afternoon and the skies were darkening. The remains of drizzle formed fragile curtains like long eyelashes, restricting the view to the village. As soon as the boat entered the village, the woman's cries subsided. She could not bear to imagine which one of her family members would be condemned to pay for the spell as a consequence of her husband's decision. Four sons had dwelled in her womb; one by one they had each died abruptly. After that she lost her own mother. Now which child would she have to sacrifice? She blamed all these losses on her husband for carrying out the bamboo-cutting ritual.

It was one of the secret rituals that had been passed down by his ancestors, a family initiation that he was prohibited from sharing with anyone except his own family members, those of the same blood or from the same womb. Only suitable adults could be told about it. It could not be carried out lightly. Even when a part of the family knew about it, only one or two family members were permitted to practice this sacred rite. Since the woman was an outsider who had become a part of her husband's family through marriage, the consequences of guarding that secret automatically fell upon her.

If his wife ever revealed the secret, she would pay with her own life – or those of her siblings who had been born from the same womb. The person to execute the sanctions for breaking this law would not be her husband, nor would it be her husband's younger or older siblings, or her husband's ancestors. It would be carried out by some being who held the highest power over the very breath of their lives. That was why each initiation performed would undoubtedly result in a victim. But they had to be prepared to pay the price. No wonder the woman had been so wretched to see her husband once more carrying out that ritual earlier in the day.

Of her eight children only four were still alive, three boys and a girl. The other four she had lost as sacrificial lambs at a very young age – as with her youngest, a one-month-old baby, who fell asleep in perfect health never to wake up again. It was never known for whom the sacrifice of that baby was designed. Her husband never spoke about it. But she had witnessed the wrath of her husband's ancestors after a family argument about land rights in the village, land that was owned by his grandfather.

The opposition – those who had forced their way in to take over the village lands over three generations – were nearly all dead now, swallowed up by the madness of that ritual. Luckily there was a smart elder who understood, and he had advised the few remaining members of the offending family to leave as soon as they could. There were only two of them, and they had packed their belongings in a rush and quickly fled – where to, no one knew. Their abandoned village had now become like an old graveyard and was a frightening place.

# Living on the Sea Shore

The woman was once more slumped in the canoe, while her husband paddled strongly. His face was harsh. His eyes were sharp and sure. The wrinkles of his face, and the black hair that stood out from his two prominent cheek bones, seemed to describe an unshakeable firmness of spirit and a disciplined attitude to life.

He was the last of the generation that had missed out on compulsory schooling. When the Malay teachers and representatives of the Europeans visited every village and pleaded with parents to let their children be educated at school, he was never to be found at home. He was always away with his father, heading for the wilds – the hunting grounds or out at sea.

But this man was aware that a person who didn't go to school was by no means lacking in knowledge. Going to that school meant learning the teachings of the white people. His grandfather had left him with a piece of wisdom. 'You also have to learn in the village – it's your responsibility. Go to school to protect the village and ancestral inheritance,' he said. His status was confirmed when his father decided to pass the teachings of the ancestors on to him.

Two of his brothers who'd had the chance to go to public school had long since migrated to the big city and never returned. Back then, when World War II ended, they had joined a crew recruited to work in the city. At first he, too, had been asked to join them by the *karani*, the man who was seeking labourers; but one night before their departure, the spirit of his late father came to him and invited him to accompany him by canoe into the jungle.

In the forest they met up with his grandfather, who had just defeated a wild boar. His catch was sprawled at the edge of the beach. He saw that his grandfather had a wound on his leg. Blood poured out, creating a puddle at the water's edge. Hurriedly the grandfather was helped on board, and the hunter's prey lifted into the canoe. On the way home, the wild boar that they had thought was dead started to struggle and rage. The wild boar's sharp tusk pierced the wall of the canoe.

Water rapidly filled the canoe and it sank. He and his father were not able to help the grandfather. They tried to dive down and chase him on the bottom of the sea, but grandfather and the canoe had both disappeared. The man could only call out and plead with his father. But by that time his father was nowhere to be seen.

When he woke up, he heard his mother calling him. To convince himself that he'd only been dreaming, he stayed still for a while, before joining his mother next to the fire. He didn't have the heart to tell her about his dream because she was already in tears. He knew that she was already grieving for her sons who were about to leave her.

As they were already adult men, their mother did not have the right to forbid them to travel abroad. She only knew that it was her responsibility to provide them with enough food. He could see her smoking their provisions at the fireplace, and he knew that just before dawn she would put the food in woven *aderi* bags.

Their clothes had already been packed in their woven palm-leaf *faiya* baskets. When the *karani* labour recruiter came to pick them up, he spoke their praises in order to gladden their mother's heart. He was a respected person in the village, who claimed to understand why the white people wanted to teach them. He had travelled and been educated by Malay and Dutch teachers at the *Sekolah Biasa* as well at the JVVS Dutch school. That was how he learned to communicate with them in their own language. When World War II ended in the Pacific, the Dutch government proclaimed the town of Hollandia, an old missionary post, as their capital, and the *karani* was given the task to find volunteers to work there. Those who had not been to school were enrolled as daily workers. Throngs of villagers were loaded onto the ship to go to the city. The youth who were tempted by the enticing possibilities of modern life lined up to enlist.

When the *karani* arrived with two of his brothers, the younger man was nowhere to be seen.

'He just left a message,' said his mother.

'But his name is on the list,' said one of the brothers.

'Mama, what did he say?' the *karani* interrupted.

'When it was still dark,' said the mother, 'he picked up his canoe paddle and I asked him, "Aren't you going away with the others?" He said, "But who's going to look after you?"'

'Now where has he paddled off to?' asked a brother.

'He must have paddled to his Tete's garden – where else?'

'Should we follow him to the island?'

'Let him be, I'll pick him up next time, when the ship returns,' said the *karani*.

Then the three of them went off to the port in a canoe. A crowd of people had gathered there. Distant relatives from neighbouring villages had also enlisted to work as labourers in the city.

The villagers were transported by motorboat to Serui. There, every worker got a health check-up, signed a contract and was then allowed to board the ship. There was a group of workers headed for Sorong. Along the way, the ship stopped in Manokwari. Some of the volunteers stayed on there to work as clerks or as labourers for the Manokwari trading fleet.

In the town of Sorong, those who were educated were placed to work in government offices. But most of them took jobs in a petroleum company that was famous at the time, Nederlandsche Nieuw Guinea Petroleum Maatschappij, known as NNGPM. The ship left Serui and headed east toward Hollandia, which was being developed into the capital city at the time.

Hollandia was the name given by the Dutch, who were working far away from their homeland. Before that it had been known as Numbay. Missionaries had turned it into a post for Bible-teaching. From this gospel-preaching post emerged the name Port Numbay. At that time it was not only Dutch missionaries who stopped by the port, but also merchants, bird-of-paradise hunters and antiques collectors.

As the ship departed from the town of Serui, the old people and relatives were left standing on the dock. Nobody moved away. Unable to cope with their sadness, some hid their faces. Some just bowed their heads. The unimaginable had happened. Suddenly the world that surrounded them, the world that was so close, had stretched far away. That first wave of workers filling the early pages of migratory history was made up of the young men of all the more accessible villages from the northern shores of the island of Papua.

When the ship's whistle blew, the *karani* puffed out his chest and tried to lift up their spirits: '*Ayo*, come on ... what happened to your voices, children of the sea? Hit by a storm? Spattered in the ocean foam? Children of Mambri, you are now standing in the front ranks of your people. Conquerors of slavery, where's your pride? It's time for you to lift your heads and stamp your feet! Beat the drum! Once the *tobura* conch shell is blown the direction will not change. This is our chance, children of the moon. If we are afraid of the high tide, we shouldn't build our homes by the sea.'

Come on! Children! Show us how brave you are!

# Mandohi Pastoral

The sun was about to set on the ocean's surface. The light shone brightly, reflecting in the water with glass-like glimmers adorned with yellow. Andevavait the tidepool blenny was stunned witnessing this, the sheer beauty of nature.

It was weird: every time he reached the end of his fasting, something magical always appeared to him, some gift of almighty nature, such as the glimmering of mist and foam in the waves at the edge of the sea as they raced for the shore at the edge of a quiet village. The rumbling waves and rustling wind left their message on the tips of the coconut palms and beach hibiscus trees in this place where the sun always took his leave at the end of the day.

By the time darkness had blanketed the beach and ocean, the distant sound of voices singing in chorus would well up, sounds of singing and dancing, joyful shouts and cheers. From that same place there sometimes came the distant melody of a traditional folk song.

Sometimes it arrived in a slow tempo, but then it slowly changed rhythm to form jerking beats full of angst and restlessness. Usually after midnight those sounds would soften once again, calm down then disappear altogether, swallowed by the sound of the crashing waves. Sometimes, as the morning star rose, the songs would turn into a lament, a truly heart-breaking expression of grief from the elder women.

At other times restless and agitated songs would come from the wooden churches. Rising together from the churches, they made it sound like a great party was in progress, high above the altars, where the god's ball of fire regularly dropped from the sky. In those moments the people wouldn't care – they just kept on dancing, singing and having fun. In the end, their voices would speak a thousand languages together, none of which could be understood by the ocean creatures or other beings that live above the water.

Andevavait's eyes glistened with tears. He was speechless. He felt he must be grateful for having been created and thankful for his existence as an amphibian who could complete – even fill – the gaps within his world. How perfect was the work of the almighty Creator! Every time he witnessed the beauty of the sky, he wondered about the power that created it. That was where the majesty of creation vibrated with all its millions of stars. The clearer the heart, the deeper its meaning, and the more ecstatic the wind, the breath of the gods.

As Andevavait the tidepool blenny contemplated his fate, he decided he had no choice but to give in completely and follow the direction his life was leading him – especially if he recalled the happy moments spent with his family, or playing and joking with his fellow inhabitants in this slippery rocky area. He recalled the saga of Raukahi the octopus losing his home because of interfering hands. As he listened to Raukahi's story, he hadn't been able to speak of the feelings in his heart. A similar disaster had caused the death of his entire family.

He imagined what would have happened then if he had not been in a dry place; he would surely be dead as well. How ferocious had been the shockwaves of the explosion of sulphur and gunpowder! He remembered the poisonous smoke and black froth clotted over the water's surface. This was the habitat of every member of Andevavait's family, with not a single exception. Those under the water at the time had met the same fate as described by the octopus.

And those who were above the water's surface couldn't dive and couldn't breathe, and eventually died because the entire water's surface was covered in the black foam of death. Andevavait and Anggereai had been luckier, saving themselves, high up on the top of the coconut palm. It was there that they witnessed the horrible incident.

Let it be. What had happened will always be remembered among friends, so that they will learn to be more careful and quickly pass on information if they spot more people intent on destroying the underwater world with dynamite or poison.

A ray of coloured shadow darkened the horizon. Even the darkness was perfect. Andevavait had been peeping at the feasting scavenger fish. He slowly edged his way back and then hastily skimmed along the water's surface, where he ran into Raukahi the octopus again.

'*Wah*, such good luck!' said Raukahi with relief. 'I'm so happy you could come back.'

'Sorry, I'm a little late. I haven't found Anggereai and Andawai yet.'

'Andev, please help me. I don't think I can continue this fasting.'

'How can you give up so soon?'

'Without you, I would have surely given up already.'

'Why, my friend?'

'I'm being terrorized!'

'By whom?'

'I'm not sure. But I'm beginning to think it might be Andawai the triggerfish.'

'Really? Tell me how he's terrorizing you.'

'He keeps knocking on the stone at the base of this coral. Then he snaps his teeth over and over again.'

'Oh, no wonder. It looks like Andawai wants confirmation from you, whether you want his help building a home.'

'Not necessarily,' said the octopus.

'Look, if he's scratching the sand and his solid snout is pounding the rock wall, it means he wants to show off his ability.'

'Ability in what?'

'Ransacking the ground and the sand, breaking down the reef, making holes to hide in.'

'Oh, of course!'

'But remember, as a reward for his hard work, you have to be prepared to pay a high price.'

'That's what makes me so nervous. I don't know what to do. I still don't understand his character or what he wants.'

'Tell me again, what did the knocking sound like?'

'I was too nervous. I don't remember how it went.'

'Never mind. I'm just guessing, but perhaps Andawai wants to meet up with you.'

'I'm too scared to meet him by myself.'

'Then I'll go with you.'

'Really? When?'

'Tomorrow afternoon, when the tide is low. I'll be waiting at the usual spot.'

'*Wah*, in that case, thanks for your help, Andev. But do you think Andawai is still around or has he gone away?'

'If he knows that I'm here, he will surely have gone away.'

'Why would he do that?'

'He'd be embarrassed because he has already been disturbing you. Now, I'm going to try to check out Andawai's hiding place.'

# Personal Naivety

In the dark, Andevavait plunged into the coldness of the water. His body slipped through a group of *kambutir* fish that was gathered in the shadow of the reef's coral. It wasn't long before he was back to see Raukahi the octopus. But it was not just news about Andawai the triggerfish that he brought with him. This time Andevavait offered his friend a package of tidily wrapped leaves.

'Some provisions to break your fast with!'
'What's in it?'
'Something to eat!'
'From Andawai?'
'No! Andawai was not at his place.'
'So …?'
'This is some food that I had put aside for another day.'
'But I'm still fasting!'
'You should break your fast after midnight,' said Andevavait.

The food was kept below water? That's weird, thought the octopus.

'It comes from the coconut tree, but I kept it in a hole in the rock, under the water.'

Having answered the octopus's query, the tidepool blenny took up his position facing the sunset. There he remained, still and quiet. Meanwhile the octopus examined the contents of the leaf package. His attention moved back toward Andevavait, but this time the swift little blenny ignored him.

After a while a swarm of mosquitoes began to make Raukahi restless. When he saw that Andevavait was still ignoring him, the octopus moved toward the rock's edge and extended two of his tentacles into the water and splashed his body.

Andevavait saw that the octopus was able to overcome his difficulties with the mosquitoes, so he impulsively decided to find a solution for something else that had been on his mind for a while. In one jerk, Andevavait slipped into the water and glided back toward the octopus.

When he was at Raukahi's side, Andevavait said to him, 'It looks like we're safe for the time being. While we wait for you to break your fast, we can chat and share our experiences.'

'Yes, Andev, but ...' The octopus looked nervous He peeped out, peering left and right, as if he was afraid of something.

'What's the matter? Are you still afraid of that gang of mosquitoes?'

'No!'

'Relax, friend. I can tell if there are any dangerous threats in this area. For now on you should just take it easy, although we should stay alert.'

'What do you mean take it easy?'

Just then there was a sudden sound of wings flapping, and a rush of strong wind blasted the heads of Andevavait and the octopus.

Spontaneously they both lay down flat and in a flash they disappeared under the water. Andevavait's eyes were the first to poke out again. His eyeballs shone, rolling round and round, splashed by ripples. Then the octopus also appeared, creeping slowly, and after a while the two of them moved back to where they'd been.

Andevavait sighed, and didn't say a word. For a few moments the two of them remained silent. Each waited to see who would make the first comment about what had just happened. They were wide awake, their faces nervous, both still searching, glancing to the left and right. They looked up, and then, both at once, they saw something.

A black figure seemed to be hanging above them from a branch of a coconut palm.

Hovering in the shadow of the branch, the black creature stared at them with blinking red eyes. Eyes like glowing coals.

Heavens! Their hearts stopped.

Before they could blink, a strange hard object fell, slicing into the water, almost hitting Andevavait and the octopus. At the same instant, the creature above broke loose, spreading its wide wings, and dived at them. The sea creatures instantly plunged back into the water, to the safety of their natural environment in the sea.

When he finally appeared above the water again, Andevavait could no longer hold back his feelings of amusement and regret. Sniffling and coughing with mixed emotions, he cursed himself for his reaction to the flying creature who he now realized was no other than Ayadiru, the fruit bat.

'I am such an idiot! That's who it was, that flying thief! What an idiot I am!'

Raukahi the octopus returned to the surface of the water, his body still trembling. He was confused and amazed to see Andevavait carrying on so. The octopus sulked. He was cold, exhausted and extremely hungry. Instinctively he looked for the leaf packet of food that Andevavait had given him. It was gone. There was nothing to do but resign himself to losing it. But he didn't want to respond to any of Andevavait's antics.

Then a question crossed his mind. How was it that someone who seemed to know more about everything and who had so much experience, could behave so naively in the eyes of others? To the point of even measuring success by his own yardstick? Sometimes, he decided, even from a self-righteous point of view, things could be accomplished only by exerting self-control and staying on course.

He thought about it for a while. It was pretty good, actually, the wisdom that he had picked up in this short life, through spending time with Andevavait.

# The Sower of Seeds

It seemed as if just a few moments had passed. Raukahi the octopus watched Andevavait the tidepool blenny as he tried his best to push something from within the water to the edge of the stone. A heavy darkness was falling, and Raukahi could not see what was floating and rolling in the water. Now he could hear Andevavait, who was in a flurry and gasping for breath, asking him for help.

'Raukahi, my friend, come give me a hand with this! Help me, will you?'

But the octopus chose to completely ignore him. Raukahi closed his eyes and pretended to be asleep. Then he heard Andevavait jump onto the stone right beside him. He kept his eyes tightly closed and waited to see what his lively friend would do. At that moment all he could feel was drops of water on his wound. Suddenly his fears and aches came back, and by reflex his eyes opened.

There was Andevavait, just about to bring his sharp fin down above the cut tentacle. Realizing the octopus had woken, Andevavait pulled his fin higher as if he was about to plunge it directly into the wound.

'Don't! Stop! Stop, I beg you! Don't!'

'Ah, you are just waking up! Here I am half dead and asking for help, and you pretend to sleep and ignore me!'

'Yes, Andev, I will help … I'll help you!'

'Come on, it's time to end your fast. Here is a bit of good luck that has fallen from the sky!' Andevavait pointed at the thing floating beside the stone.

'Good luck? What do you mean?' said Raukahi.

'You have all those long tentacles, what are you waiting for, come on, pull that thing up here!'

'What is it?'

'Don't ask silly questions, just help me.' Andevavait jumped back into the water and pushed the object. It was a mango.

Raukahi stretched out four tentacles and wrapped them around the fruit. The other three tentacles held on tightly to the edge of the stone. Andevavait pushed from within the water. Finally the mango that had been nudged by the bat was manoeuvred into a dry place.

'Now please break your fast. I am tired and wish to rest.'

Andevavait left Raukahi facing the mango. The fruit exuded a sweet aroma. Carefully examining this thing that was said to have fallen from the sky, the octopus noticed the marks of a bite left on the mango. The aroma of the fruit seemed strange to him, but he was sorely tempted to taste it.

'Just the smell of it makes me feel hungry. But, Andev, I've never eaten this fruit before!'

'That's why you should please try it now. Eat until you are completely satisfied,' Andevavait answered, rather annoyed.

'Just now you said it fell from the sky?'

'*Wah*, are you going to eat it or what?'

'But there's a bite mark on the fruit. Was it that big bat who knocked it down?'

'Ayadiru the *paniki* is not the devil! That fellow up there next to the sun, the one who dropped the fruit, he's just a bat!' Andevavait said crossly.

'Enough! I'm not going to touch this thing.' The octopus moved away from the mango fruit.

'Oh, so you wish to continue your fast, my friend?'

Without waiting for a reply from the octopus, Andevavait went to the mango and without the slightest effort peeled it, and started to bite into at the same spot where the bat had left off. He ate it in a relaxed manner, glancing from time to time at Raukahi, who remained silent.

If this goes on too long, thought Andevavait, he would soon start feeling sorry for his friend. After all, he had only been here for a short time and he was used to living under the surface of the water, so it made sense if he had never met a creature of the night such as the bat. Even his experience of daylight hours was very limited, so he couldn't really blame the octopus for behaving like this.

'Come on, my friend, let's eat it together,' said Andevavait, encouraging Raukahi to join him. But Raukahi seemed genuinely uninterested, although he could hardly bear his hunger. So Andevavait began to talk.

'The *paniki* is a fruit bat. He's actually treated by the local people here as if he were one of their own family. According to the stories of the elders in the village here, he's a member of their family who has been exiled to live his life alone.' Andevavait paused, and then went on eating his breakfast. The octopus still did not respond, so Andevavait continued.

'It's quite sad, really, if you think about the fate of Ayadiru the *paniki*. People think of him only as a nocturnal creature. They think he has nothing better to do than to stay up all night, stealing from their gardens and yards. When dawn comes he hurries home to his stone cave, where he dwells. People are afraid of him with his skinny body and haggard face and red eyes.'

At that moment the octopus edged closer to Andevavait and began to listen to him seriously. Andevavait pretended not to notice and carried on.

'The grandmothers in the village often remind their grandchildren what to do if, in the middle of the night, they have a guest who flaps his wings in the garden or yard. They advise them to leave him alone. "That is our family member who is visiting to take his share of what is rightfully his," they say. "He flaps his wings as a mark of respect, or to ask for permission. Our relative is only living out his fate, as the sower of the seed. He never complains and he never makes demands. He is the sower who never hoards and never thinks of making a profit. He sows and gathers for everyone. He spreads seeds along the beach, sowing between islands, along the entire length of the land and continents."' Andevavait paused.

'Why did you stop?' Raukahi asked.

'Why did I stop eating the mango?' replied Andevavait.

'No. Keep talking about Ayadiru, I ... I like it!'

'Right. Why don't you join me and enjoy the meat of this mango?'

'Thank you, Andev.' Finally the octopus was willing to try Andevavait's gift.

'How does it taste, my friend?'

'Amazing, no wonder ...' Raukahi didn't continue, he just shook his head in delight.

'What do you think? Delicious, isn't it?'

'No wonder you forgot to carry on telling the story about the bat!'

'Ah, yes. Never mind. Listen, my friend. It is almost midnight. We have to hurry up and hide in the stones. You keep the rest of the mango for tomorrow night.'

'What about the bat?'

'I'll continue the story after we are safely hidden in the stones. And don't forget about Andawai the triggerfish. I feel sure that soon after dawn tomorrow Andawai will appear. And that means you may soon have your own house. A safe place free of all threats.'

'Really? Thank you, Andev!'

# Magic of the Morning Star

Bright flecks in stony depths
The tide leaves watery footprints
Broken coral
Cracked fruit of the *mandong*
Brilliant green sea-grass
trembling seaweed hair.

A half moon becomes a blue jellyfish
Its sword of love revealing a honeyed tip
Shy and naked.
The lingam – firm, rigid,
flying like a holy banner.
He inhales the womb's fragrance
and thus
leaves the last embers of lust at stone lips.
The night is full of stars and
the wind no longer blusters.

Even the *worar* and *wawaru* trees are lulled.
The shore so desolate
as quiet as the song of Ai-reng,
as sad as the crab-warrior Anggarariti
digging a living grave
fashioning a trap

of foamy water,
stinging his lips at every mouthful.

His breath chases the cloud chariots
as he stretches himself gracefully,
and creeps up the hill
toward the top of the smouldering night.
There he looks back over his shoulder,
scratching
scratching till bleeding
blood trickles into a million tattooed holes
where he brushes and strokes the ocean's hair
lulled and arriving,
swept away too soon.

# Night Mystery

When he woke up, Raukahi the octopus found himself alone, and there was no sign of Andevavait the tidepool blenny. Suddenly Raukahi felt worried about the condition of his broken body, it was such a mess. He felt as if he had just awoken from a dream. Something strange had happened to him. He tried to remember: was it the previous night that Andevavait had plied him with drinks? He still remembered the moment that Andevavait had wanted to dance with him, and from then on his memory was blank.

At that moment Andevavait arrived, smiling to see that Raukahi was already awake.

'Hi, how are you feeling?' Andevavait greeted him.

'Hi! Oh dear, I feel so embarrassed ... How can I explain?'

'Just calm down and relax,' said Andevavait.

'It's easy for you to say that, but you cheated!'

'*Wah*, I cheated? What's the matter?'

'Never mind. I just want to go home!!'

'It's still early – what's the hurry?'

Suddenly Raukahi spread his tentacles, closing the exit.

'Before I go, I want to ask you – what did you give me to drink last night? And after I started to feel dizzy, you hugged me and I lost consciousness. What did you do to me?'

'We were drinking together and we both got dizzy,' said Andevavait.

'And then?'

'And then I starting singing.'

'And then?'

'You joined in and sang along with me!'

'Hmm!'

'I asked you to dance,' said Andevavait.

'No! You were hugging me!'

'Because you were staggering.'

'That's a lie!'

'That's truly what happened.'

'That's not possible. I wouldn't fall over. I never even stood up!'

The octopus was getting angry. He spread his tentacles out in a circle, then wrapped them around Andevavait's body and began to tighten his grip.

Andevavait felt threatened, but he did not lose control. He responded quickly.

'My friend, at this moment Andawai is waiting for us outside. I came to let you know, so that you can discuss the plans for your house.'

'No, Andev! First answer my question!'

'What question do you have for me now?'

'What was the drink that you served me last night?'

'Oh that! It was *je anggadi*, a drink made from the coconut palm.'

'How did you get hold of it?'

'That's my business.'

'Yes, but where and how did you get it?'

'That's a secret. You are just like the Intel – secret police!'
'Who is the Intel?'
'My friend Anggereai.'
'And so?'
'And so what!'
'Tell me, where did you get that drink?'
'I told you already, that's my business!'

Raukahi tightened his hold and Andevavait began to feel truly distressed.

'I'm not going to tell you.'
'Now tell me: after you cuddled me what were you going to do?'
'At that moment, I was truly startled.'
'Why?'
'Because ... because it turned out that you were not a male, as I had always assumed.'
'If I was not a male, why did you keep on embracing me?'
'Ah, come on, you know you didn't faint. In fact you returned my embrace.'
'Ichh!'

# A Faceless Guest

A rowdy noise could be heard outside their place of hiding. Andevavait used the opportunity to escape from Raukahi's tentacles, and the octopus did not prevent his exit. But as soon as he was invited to meet Andawai the triggerfish, Raukahi wouldn't budge. He refused to go out. It was now Andevavait's turn to be confused.

'Come on,' urged Andevavait, 'it's time for us to remind Andawai of his promise.'

'If I don't want to, what's it to you?'

'Don't be like that.'

'You remind Andawai of his promise on your own.'

'This is in your interest, it's important for your safety.'

'But right now I feel a lot safer staying right here.'

'So you don't want to go home?'

'Home to where? I want to keep fasting, forever, right here.'

'Until doomsday ...!'

'Let me be!'

'Oh, for goodness sake ... Now I'm serious. I will go to meet Andawai. What should I tell him?'

Raukahi did not reply. Andevavait quickly went out – but Andawai and his retinue of scavenger fish were nowhere to be seen. All he could see was a canoe from the village that had been pulled up on the beach. The man and his woman had left their canoe there, but Andevavait couldn't see them anywhere.

Andevavait crossed over to a stone that was closer to the edge of the water, but he was so shocked by what he saw that he quickly hid. The man was standing like a statue on the rock, guarding it with his *aringgoya*, a stabbing device made from a piece of bamboo with a sharp piece of wire at the lower end. The man was so relaxed his eyes did not even blink. It was as if he was not even breathing. If any other creature had passed by, he surely would not have noticed him there. Andevavait kept peeping from behind the stone, observing every intake of breath the man took. Then with a very slow movement, the man aimed his *aringgoya* spear at a target, and in a flash the spear was launched. The surface of the water flared up, and the man held tight to the end of his piece of bamboo.

Suddenly someone leapt down from the coconut palm and dived on the prey, followed closely by a child who appeared from behind the palm tree, shouting gleefully. The man who had leapt into the water had captured Ubokahoi, the big *bandeng* whitefish who was as large as a man's thigh. They took the fish to the beach and dropped it floundering on the sand. All three people stood around the flapping Ubokahoi with a satisfied expression on their faces, watching till he eventually stopped moving. The elder man then repaired the barb of his *aringgoya*. The steel wire had become bent in the process.

The man who captured Ubokahoi hauled him to the edge of the stone and began cutting him up. The surface of the water turned red. A passing entourage of scavenger fish inherited all the off-cuts as well as the contents of Ubokahoi's stomach. They got all the leftover bits except for the heart of the fish, which was wrapped in a leaf and put aside. The festive debauchery of the scavenger fish continued happily. The little boy took a toy spear and posed just like his father had done, waiting to choose his prey amongst the uninvited guests who were feasting on the remains.

In another corner of the feasting place, unknown to others, another pair of eyes was watching, without joining in the feasting frenzy.

The older man gathered up dried branches, and soon smoke started to billow forth. Once the fire gave way to hot coals, the pieces of Ubokahoi's flesh would be roasted. The smoke and the aroma from the fireplace acted as a signal to more unexpected guests. Just like a fishy smell in the water, the smoke and the smell of roasting in the air could turn into a feast, or perhaps the opposite.

From his hiding place, Andevavait counted the number of guests who showed up. From Amumar, the moon wrasse, Kowar the Whitley's sergeant, Uneng the yellow-margined sea perch, Kikou the black-spotted sea perch, Kerephuni the sharp-nosed wrasse, Muantonang the thumbprint emperor, Bitowahi the butterfly fish, Nyawaiker the long green wrasse, Ampampurem the pale-striped cardinal fish, Awesuain the peacock rock cod, Maraiberar the triple-tail Maori wrasse, Rurui the crimson soldierfish, Woriawa the blue-ringed angelfish, Moridai the spinefoot, Aremetang the golden-lined spinefoot, Amperung the crescent perch, and Tabeawa the batfish, right up to Nuai the scorpion fish and Rawedain the stuck-up firefish, who was just like a peacock, with his flamboyant fins and the startling beauty of his physique.

At the surface of the water a group of *ainai* Endracht hardyheads pushed and shoved each other forward. On the deep outside edge, a school of *ansanai* flat-tailed longtoms were seeking an opportunity to get their share. Not to be left behind, Tawaiseng the coral eel and Andawai the red-striped triggerfish now joined in.

Andevavait noted Andawai's presence. He had not kept his rendezvous. Maybe because it was a feast, Andawai had forgotten his promise. But Andevavait recalled that Andawai had often disappeared somewhere, and nobody ever seemed to know where he had gone.

Among all the scavengers, only Anggereai the amphibious crab had not shown up, even though the *anggarariti* crab family and the *kawein* lobster family were represented, and even the ancient *mambara-kamiai* brown-banded cat sharks had shown up, along with the stonefish, Gorano, and they all joined in the feast. Everyone was there except Bohurai the toadfish, who was still fasting. And of Anggereai the crab? Where could he be, this one missing friend? Andevavait hoped that Anggereai had not met the same fate as the unfortunate crab Aiweirori.

As mentioned in the previous story, Andevavait had last met Anggereai the amphibious crab at a moment when Bohurai the toadfish was feeling extremely sleepy. In fact the crab had just woken him up, and then returned to his former position, so he could keep an eye upon Bohurai, in case he did anything odd. At first Anggereai wanted to report to the others about Bohurai's strange behaviour, but at that time Andevavait was too tired to listen. Later on Anggereai himself was able to watch the behaviour of the toadfish. But then the husband and wife from the village had shown up, and Anggereai lost his focus. He decided to watch what the village couple were up to instead, just as he had done before when the wife was digging up coral and the husband cut a piece of bamboo and performed a ceremony with it.

When the woman cried out in protest at her husband carrying out the ritual, Anggereai quickly jumped from the top of the stone and swam in the direction of the boat that was tied up on the beach. He wanted to get a better spot to watch the scene. But from this new position at the edge of the water, he found his view blocked by terraces of sand. Anggereai then crawled right up onto the boat. From this new spot he could see the unfolding events much more easily. When the woman was dragged and thrown into the boat, Anggereai became even more determined to record what happened. The moments when the boat was pushed into the sea and the man spoke loudly in the direction of the coconut tree were also recorded in his memory, along with the long journey in the boat to the village.

He even witnessed the goings-on at night at the home of the boat people. Then the following day at dawn they headed back to their garden with the crab still on board. Not with the woman, however: now there were two new passengers on board.

The question Andevavait needed to know the answer to was, had Anggereai actually come all the way back with them? Who could tell! And where on earth was Anggereai now?

There is something we should keep in mind, however: Anggereai the amphibious crab is always faithful to his responsibilities as a reporter and a witness.

# The Stealing of *Je Anggadi*

Smoke was wafting up into the air. Chunks of *ubokahoi* meat were laid out on the leaves of the *ketapang* sea-almond tree as soon as the smoke became fire. As he waited for the fire to turn into coals, a young man took some raw sago out of his string *aderi* bag, made from the fibre of the bark of the *wawaru* beach hibiscus. He piled the sago onto three leaves from the *tawaang* tree and then wrapped them around it in triangular shapes. When the fire started to burn well, he set the packets of sago directly on top.

Meanwhile the young man climbed the coconut palm to complete his unfinished business, slicing the virgin coconut shoots so they would drip sap into the bamboo cylinder known as *mamurang*. The following day, the bamboo tube would surely be full. Then the bamboo and its contents could be removed, the same shoot would be cut once more, and yet another empty *mamurang* fixed in its place.

Later, the same routine would be repeated regularly, until the final cut had been made at the base of the shoot, before moving to another, or to the next coconut palm. This procedure would be carried out for as long as the owner of the coconut grove allowed. But if he decided to produce coconuts, the slicing of the coconut shoots must be discontinued. If on each tree just one shoot is left to blossom and become fruit, while the other shoots are cut so as to be milked of their sap for toddy, it will affect all the other fruit, causing the coconuts to wilt in their early stages and drop off.

After placing the bamboo in the top of the cut into the shoot, the young man was ready to descend. But his hand that was holding onto the frond of the palm tree touched something that moved, startling him, and he lost his grip. Luckily his other hand, which held the machete, quickly grabbed another branch and saved him from falling. But the machete fell free, along with the body of a crab that glided alongside it, falling directly into the water.

At that moment Andevavait could catch only a brief signal, but it sounded to him like a call from Anggereai. By the time he peeped back up at the tree, he saw that his friend Anggereai was only just now managing to jump down after his fellow crab who had fallen first. Andevavait didn't respond immediately, as the man was rushing to get down the tree and would at any minute dive in after his machete. Andevavait was confused as to why there should be another, slightly different figure leaping down with Anggereai. He decided to be patient and just observe whatever happened next.

When he got to the bottom of the tree, the man was about to leap into the water, but he changed his mind, as the boy had already jumped in ahead of him and was now swimming towards the edge, brandishing the machete above the water. When he got to the shore, the boy went up to the man, who was still grimacing with anger. The man smiled at his son and then cursed the small animals that had caused his machete to fall into the water.

'*Aishee … wau, anta isobu wau manii* … If only I had caught you,' he said to the machete, 'that would not have happened.'

He took the machete from the boy. Then as they headed back together to join the old man, he continued surreptitiously cursing under his breath as if still angry with himself.

'Ah, what a pity, if only I had caught you that would not have happened!' he said again loudly, so the child would hear it. Perhaps he wished to compliment the boy's bravery.

# A Breath of Tradition

Amid the smoke and the aroma of the grilling fish, the face of the older man lost its worried look and relaxed into its usual solemn expression. When he began to speak, it seemed that he was no longer just addressing his younger brother and the boy. There could have been a crowd of people gathered there. He rambled on as he grilled the fish, replacing the cooked pieces with raw fish. First he commented upon the carelessness of his younger brother, who had not been cautious enough when he was at the top of the coconut palm. Then he directed his scolding towards the village people, who had all begun to be very careless of late. 'Too lazy to work in their own village,' he said, 'they prefer to rely on the hard work of other people.' Finally he added, 'they're becoming accustomed to helping themselves to the property of others.'

Hunting in other people's villages and stealing from other people's gardens, according to him, was taboo, because their ancestors had ruled it so. It was their tradition to always value and protect other people's property, and especially nature, the animals and birds in the forest. Every plant, tree, or bit of scrub had the right to live and had its own guardian. There were also sacred and magical values to consider. They had links and dependencies and mutually beneficial relationships with each other.

'If we think clean and play fair with nature,' he told them, 'then nature will open its secrets to us.

'According to our ancestors, as intelligent beings we must

value other people and the natural world. That's why the ancestors left us with traditions to guide us in our daily life,' he went on. 'In order to keep the balance, we must have a system of reward and punishment, teaching lessons to those who purposely or accidentally destroy the order and norms of balance – so that those who are able to see and hear will not repeat the same mistakes. Then there will be no stealing from others, no dishonesty.'

Without looking at the faces of the young man and the boy, the old man stopped talking and invited them to eat. They each took a wrapped triangle of grilled sago. Then the old man took half of the fish head and moved aside. The boy was hesitant and waited to be encouraged before he would begin eating. The father watched his son dotingly. He considered him his eldest child, because the boy's three elder brothers had all died. Sometimes, when he was sitting alone and watching the behaviour of his son, his heart felt like it would break and his eyes would fill with tears. But he never allowed his wife or his children to see how he felt.

Once, the man's younger brother had seen him grieving. Sometimes he would chant to himself as he paddled his canoe. He would repeat the names of the places, the mountains and the coastal promontories. One by one he would count the plants that lined the beach, as if they were virgin girls or hotshot men, and the heroic warlords known as *mambri* in his dialect. He would remember back, counting his old friends and relatives who had left long ago, painting once more the picture of those moments when they were young together, playing together, struggling, hunting and capturing their prey in the forest or the sea, sailing the coastal waters and exploring new places. At those moments his eyes would fill with tears, as if he had caught the reflection of the sunlight mirrored on the surface of the water.

Chanting and paddling brought the many miles of distance so much closer. After a while he could imagine his son in the future, when he had grown up and become like himself. But was it necessary to give his child the heritage of the ancestors? The child was still innocent, so maybe not. There was only one other youth, his younger brother; perhaps he would be the last hope. When the time came to hand over the duty of taking care of the village, or his destiny suddenly came to fetch him, he should be ready. At least now he felt as if he had carried out the duties assigned him by his grandfather and his father.

# A Hot Heart

Anggereai the crab lifted his friend's wounded body to the top of the stone, and then laid him down on a dry spot. Drawing a deep breath, he relaxed for a moment, and then he made sure that there was no other danger threatening them. He looked toward the beach where the three villagers were enjoying their meal of grilled fish, then observed the scene over by the coconut tree where the calamity had taken place.

A feeling of guilt haunted Anggereai. It seemed that the wounded crab, a member of Anggereai's extended family, had broken his shell at the base of his leg when he fell from the coconut tree. Now the crab could only lie there and let Anggereai lick the wounds. But to mend the shattered shell, Anggereai would need to enlist Andevavait's help. Now all he could do was wait until the three people left the beach, so that Andevavait could go ashore and get some medicinal plants.

As if he already knew of Anggereai's plan, Andevavait silently appeared, just behind the stone, without being noticed by Anggereai's wounded companion. He signalled his friend to come closer.

'Who is that with you?' Andevavait whispered, not wishing to be heard by the crab with Anggereai.

Confused as to how to answer, Anggereai thought for a moment and then, with a big voice and a glance back at his friend, he said 'What luck, Andev. You've come just in time. I need your help.'

Andevavait was startled. Now Anggereai's companion knew he was there, so he moved closer.

'Oh, I'm sorry. What can I do for you?' Although he felt a bit embarrassed, Andevavait managed to compose himself.

'My friend here has had an accident and shattered an ankle! Do you know of any herbs that could fix it?'

Andevavait moved closer to the victim to check the condition of his wounds.

'What do you think, friend?' said Anggereai impatiently.

'Hold on,' said Andevavait.

Anggereai nudged Andevavait's body impatiently. 'What do you reckon?'

'Oh, what a pity!' Andevavait was still.

Anggereai tugged Andevavait aside and said, 'What do you think, my friend, can you help or not?'

Now Andevavait pulled Anggereai further away from their wounded friend. 'You scoundrel! Where did you find that female?'

Speaking in whispers, Andevavait cursed Anggereai.

Anggereai returned the abuse. 'You're a scoundrel, too! Why are you hanging around her?'

'You asked for my help, and then you wouldn't let me get close to your …'

'Friend, your methods of seeing and getting close are too offensive.' Anggereai was trying to stall him.

Now the female crab interrupted them both. 'Oh, the pain! Help me!'

Anggereai pushed Andevavait away as he tried to move closer.

'Just tell me the ingredients of the medicine, and I will medicate her myself!'

'My friend, first tell me: where did you get that female?'

'Why do you need to ask?'

'Up to you, my friend, if you don't want …'

'Yes, I want to heal her quickly. But what's the connection between the medicine and where I found her?' said Anggereai, full of suspicion.

'Precisely – it is the closeness of that connection that I need to know about!'

'And if I tell you, what then?'

'Then I will go find the right medicine.'

The female crab groaned, 'Oh, help! It hurts!'

Ignoring Andevavait, Anggereai went up to the female and began to lick the wound on her ankle. Andevavait could only watch from afar, but without realizing he edged in closer, and he reprimanded Anggereai.

'My friend, wounds of the skin or the flesh may be licked, but wounds of the shell must be wrapped with special herbs and it takes time for the shell to heal.'

Anggereai paused and looked hard at Andevavait.

'Now I leave it up to you, friend. If you want to help, I will go with you to look for the herbs for the medicine.'

Suddenly Andevavait made a signal for the others to be quiet. It looked as if the three people back on the beach were packing up and would soon pull their canoe into the water. Andevavait gazed at the *bitau* tree out on the tip of the cape. There was no sign of the kingfisher. Instead he was shocked to see a black shadow looming behind the dense foliage of the *warar* and *ampite* trees. There was another serious threat. In the meantime his view of the boat was still blocked by the sand ripples. He guessed that two strong men were not enough to carry such a heavy boat over dry land to the edge of the water. Could he rely on that guess? He figured their only choice was to wait till the tide came back in. This meant the boat wouldn't leave until later – so Andevavait's plan to seek medicinal plants was also thwarted. And the most terrifying obstacle was waiting out there for them, just beyond the dense foliage of the trees.

Then they saw a sign from the boy, who had seized his *reti*, a smaller version of the *aringgoya* fishing spear. The child stepped out onto the sand and headed toward them. Andevavait and Anggereai looked at each other. This was a bad sign. Without too much thought, Anggereai seized the female crab, who was still groaning, and dragged her into his hiding place, a gap between two stones at the edge of the cliff. Nobody else besides Andevavait knew this place. The secret dwelling could not be reached by the waves or the high tide. Even land-bound animals would find it difficult to reach, as mossy, slippery stones surrounded it.

Remembering Raukahi the octopus, Andevavait quickly moved along the gap between the stones and dived into the water. He chose to circumnavigate the outside of the cliff so that he would not meet up with the boy. Perhaps by now the boy had already arrived at the stone where they had been hiding just moments before.

From a distance Andevavait listened for Anggereai to give him a sign that the boy was coming in his direction. As he rose to the surface of the water, Andevavait kept an eye out, so that if he saw him he could dive down and try to grab his attention and lead him away. If they passed each other and the boy saw him, surely the boy would be tempted to hunt him. In this way he might manage to draw him away successfully.

Now he came to the stone where they liked to hide. Before he could check on Raukahi, Andevavait noticed the little hunter checking out the stone where Andawai the triggerfish was hiding. He studied the boy's behaviour. He did not try to pull the stone out or turn it over. His movements were extremely careful, so as not to disturb the surface of the water, allowing him to see any movements around the stone.

Now he was bending over closer to the stone. His ear was pressed close to edge of the stone wall, so that each sound that emerged from within the hollow stone would be heard by him at the surface. Andevavait suspected Andawai might give himself away, as he could never hide his extremities or his weaknesses. His teeth always chattered and clashed, sometimes without any clear reason. Perhaps the boy would hear him? This will be the end of Andawai, thought Andevavait. Then he also remembered Raukahi, and instinctively he headed back to the cave. But it as it turned out, the octopus had already taken flight.

# Masterpiece

So they were created in pairs
When he discovered himself,
ugly and black
even he denied himself
denied his body
his own flesh
his own mouth
his eyes
ears
hair
dirty
rancid.
His own rotting.
Then, he fishes among his shadows
to make another self
the two of them,
together,
then
become three
multiplying into a dozen
in the shape of a cloud,
they fill the air,
fill the moon,
block the light

land on the summit
and then gaze at the world
where there is no light.
Nothing changes colour,
rainbows hide
in monochrome... fading to black.

He protests against the creator.
Thus the ocean's riches are strewn
in their brilliance,
ten thousand flickering crowns
sprayed and scattered.

From the highest crown
one is marked.
The colours become desolate
then the words flow,
flow like blood,
riding the wind.
The living heart
flowing blue
flowing yellow
flowing black
flowing white
flowing white....

Andevavait gasped and woke up. It was if he was encountering something that he had lost of himself. He was reclining against a stony wall, at the same place where, just the night before, he and Raukahi had undergone their most unusual experience. Suddenly he felt weak, as if all the strength within his body had evaporated. The emptiness within him felt like sheer desolation.

> The space inside felt empty.
> His throat so tight
> he could barely breathe
> he could not speak.
> Emptiness engulfed him
> and touched his spirit
> Absolute desolation infused him.
> In his soul,
>     the mother manifests
> In his fervent prayers
> a burst of clouds sails in the wind
> their course penetrating the mist.
> As transparent as a saint's eyes
> the horizon glows,
> a crossing of peace,
>     washed in blue
> waters, as a face reflected
> fills the sky, floating.
> The sun rises like a king
> to guard all directions.
> The world takes flight

guarding souls that orbit the universe
to enter a womb,
for the longest prayer.

# Seven Rainbows

Now he felt his presence just as a footprint feels the earth. Slowly that footprint gave shape to an arm, and then he started to feel he was once more complete. His hand touched and grabbed hold of something. A ring!

'I hope this isn't a dream,' he thought. To Andevavait it seemed quite heavy for something as small as this. He did not know it was the accessory of a female that lived in another world altogether. And strangely enough, at that very moment he heard the sound of a woman crying. It reminded him of Raukahi the octopus. He stared closely at the ring, and then looked back at the place where he had found it. There was something else there, something octagonal that looked like a shield. At every corner of the shield was attached a chain of bead-like objects that reflected a sparkling silvery light.

'These things must belong to Raukahi,' he thought. 'But who in fact is this octopus character that has become a part of my life? And why would he leave these things lying around?'

The injured octopus was nowhere to be seen. Had he left these things on purpose as a message? Andevavait put them back where he had found them. Then he decided to search for Mr Seven-fingers right away. No matter what might happen and whoever the octopus turned out to be, he determined he must meet Raukahi.

Andevavait peeped out of the water to see if the boy was

still up there, chasing Andawai. There was nobody there. But the position of the boat had not yet changed. And the child he was so afraid of was busy piling up the remaining coals of the fire and burning the leftover fish bones. The older man and his brother were nowhere to be seen.

Andevavait kept still. He tried to remember the voice of the crying female. Surely the sound had come from the female crab, crying about the cut caused by the broken shell. He was reminded of his promise to look for medicine. But he was not going to leave until he was sure Raukahi was in a safe position. Or could it be that something had gone wrong with him? Raukahi's presence was so special, even if it was still an unsolved mystery.

Worries cause ripples. Andevavait slowly slipped over the edge of the stone until his entire body was immersed under the surface of the water. There was no sign yet of the high tide. No reason not to hug the edge of the clear water at low tide. Who knows, maybe the octopus was also missing the pleasures of his world, after having fasted for all that time and spending his time in the world above the water. Diving past the stony area, Andevavait reached the edge of the seaweed and white sand.

There he stopped, in astonishment, for he could not believe his eyes. Right there, on top of the white sand, where the water was clear and the sky was blue above, he saw the octopus sunbathing. How captivating! Raukahi's body twisted as he rinsed himself under the rays of the sun, his tentacles enchantingly graceful.

It was as if seven dancers were enacting the story of the Goddess of the Rainbow. Andevavait was charmed. Without realizing it, he swallowed some water dripping into his throat. He choked and coughed. In a flash the sky at the bottom of the sea went dark.

It was a total black out! The stage was empty!

Andevavait found himself alone, diving and looking here and there. The seven dancers seemed to have vanished behind the stage curtain.

# Mystery Cave

Andevavait was engulfed with worry. He was vexed, sad, curious, miserable and disoriented all at once. With no concern for his own safety, he mustered all his energy. He checked in all the corners, gaps and holes in the stones, all the way into the depths of the ocean where it was very cold. There he found the steep cliffs and caves in which giant fish lived. He was so desperate to find his friend that, without thinking, he entered a strange cave: he thought he might have found the hiding place of Raukahi the octopus. He entered confidently and examined every detail of the walls of the cave. Perhaps the octopus had camouflaged himself to look like a relief on the cave wall.

At the far end of the cave a door barred his way. A kind of giant valve was expanding regularly and then deflating and spreading hot air and a rotten smell along with dirty waste. No wonder there was a gathering of small scavenger fish here – *kambutir* split-banded cardinal fish and *kawariroin*. Strange, he thought: the *kawariroin* fishes usually only live between the fingers of the *ansansina* sea urchins.

It crossed Andevavait's mind that this could be the cave of a god, a place for worshipping the ancestors of the octopus. Anggereai had once told a story about such a place and described as a place of judgement. But here the marks and trail of Raukahi's movement could no longer be seen. A thing that looked like a ship's anchor was stuck in a corner of the cave, which appeared to get progressively narrower. As he got closer, the water in the cave suddenly began to tremble, and the valve opened as the mouth of the cave closed.

It was too late for Andevavait to go back. In total darkness he decided to head toward the entry door, but there was something sucking him in, and the valve was closing. All the little fishes in the cavity had been sucked in. Andevavait's body was stuck and blocking the way between the valve and the anchor. Both of his fins stuck into the soft walls of the valve.

The magic cave was the throat of Aiwa, the giant grouper.

This must be the end of me! he thought.

But Aiwa's throat was itching and suddenly the body of the giant fish shook and his tail began to wave back and forth. The cave and the coral wall rumbled, and sand and mud flew in every direction, as the entire contents of Aiwa's stomach were vomited out of the mouth of the cave. Andevavait escaped with it, turning and twisting amidst clouds of debris and water, like a spinning top.

Andevavait's glazed view caught and held the wall of the coral. When the base of the wall was clear, he moved carefully upwards, hugging the wall so that any predators who saw him would not be able to attack. Luckily, at that moment there were no predators passing by. Perhaps the noise of the broken coral falling had caused the fish to stay away. Andevavait remained focused to avoid the falling rubble. As he got close to the surface the noise grew louder, and as he passed the source of the noise his body suddenly felt like it had been caught up like a kite in the wind. By the time he reached the surface he was no longer conscious.

# Balance

Andevavait dreamt that two divers had come to him. After examining his unconscious body they gestured to each other in sign language. Then they dived and pulled his body back down to the bottom of the sea. When they got to the cave, where Aiwa the giant grouper had reclined earlier, they held him down until his body got used to the pressure. Suddenly one of the divers knocked on his aqualung with his knife. His friend, who was holding Andevavait's body, watched him and then replied with a signal, moving his hand across his neck. Then the other replied with a thumbs-up with both hands. Together they moved closer, and when they were facing each other, the diver who held Andevavait's body suddenly released his mouthpiece and gave it to his friend. The breathing mouthpiece on the end of the regulator hose was fastened over his mouth. Initially the mouthpiece was not of any use. Squeezing Andevavait's body, they moved upwards. Stopping from time to time and swapping the mouthpiece, they finally made it up to the surface.

Once he had regained consciousness and vomited, Andevavait's body was laid out on the surface of a level rock. When he came to, he was given water to drink. He felt as if he were sleeping on a soft mattress and the aroma around him reminded him of something from his childhood. He felt as if he had returned to the side of his mother. The atmosphere gently lulled his thoughts; he felt no urge to get up from his bed. He could hear the faint sound of a strange song in the distance that after a while became more and more delightful!

| SINGGAH – SINGGAH | SONG OF EXORCISM |
|---|---|
| *Kolo – singgah* | Hai, all creatures who visit in time and space |
| *Pansuminggah* | Who strive to escape |
| *Durgo kolo* | the power of death |
| *Sumingkir* | Stand aside |
| *Singo sirah* | out of my head |
| *Singo wulu* | out of my hair |
| *Singo suku* | out of my feet |
| *Singo tankasa motoo* | out of the unseen |
| *Kabhe podho,* | Return to your origins |
| *Sumingkir ...* | Stand aside ... |

Suddenly Andevavait felt as if he were seated on the wind and flying, carried by the voice of the song. High up on the wind he met a person wearing a turban. The man had a elongated nose like Winnetou, and his hair was long, covering his serene face. First the man sang a song, and then he stood up and read a number of poems on different pages, which he released one by one to be carried on the wind.

Slowly Andevavait's eyes opened. But he quickly closed them again. He was afraid the beautiful dream would end. He was afraid to return and follow his destiny as Andevavait the tidepool blenny. Then he felt his mattress beginning to move, as if he were on the stomach of a snake. Suddenly Andevavait arose. What a surprising sight greeted him: he had been lying on Raukahi's lap! The goddess of dancing just smiled; she was holding her tentacles together to form a mattress. In Andevavait's eyes this creature was so elegant. Even if her body was no longer whole, Andevavait still wanted to stretch out again on that mattress, so comforting. But he felt Raukahi retract her tentacles one by one until finally Andevavait was sitting directly on the stone. They looked at each other.

There was nothing to be said. No questions; just understanding and appreciation of each other. Raukahi, understanding the confusion he saw reflected in the eyes of Andevavait, simply smiled and nodded. Andevavait's expression reflected his spirit that had found a place to shelter. He felt like a rainbow; he had seen his mother and rediscovered himself as a child.

# The Arrival of Good Luck

The condition of the female crab was deteriorating. The torn wounds on the shell encasing her legs had resulted in an infection within the flesh. Her body temperature was heating up and she had begun to shiver. After his saliva had not been of much help, Anggereai had gone back and forth several times to check the tide, which was starting to come in. And there was still no sign of the three people on the beach making any move to go home.

In fact at that moment there was nobody to be seen, just a canoe that remained tethered on the sand. Anggereai called out to Andevavait, but there was no answer. Meanwhile the incline of the sun was increasing. Wandering back and forth in confusion, Anggereai didn't know what to do to help his female companion. He was desperate.

'I will go myself,' he thought, 'even without Andevavait, to look for the healing herbs.' And then the female crab begged him for cold water. Anggereai provided the water, but the female refused it. She wanted water from the mountain, the pure rainwater that flowed continually, and usually could be gathered at an estuary not far from there.

Anggereai scraped back the top of a dried *bitau* nut so he could use it to carry water, and crossed over toward the stream. But he returned abruptly, leaving the nut behind. He had been alarmed by a pair of *rawei* crows who were perched on the branches of a *wawaru* tree near the stream's mouth. Instead of taking a risk with those black creatures, Anggereai changed his direction and headed toward another *bitau* tree at the end of the cape. He hugged the edge of the stones as he looked for another dry nut, and then he quickly swam the rest of the way to the base of the tree. There he found a source of water that he hadn't known about. A drip from between the stones was trickling steadily into the roots of the tree. Anggereai chose the best nut he could find, cut a hole in it and placed it directly under the water drip.

His next challenge was how to get the container of water over to its destination. At that moment, Anggereai felt some debris fall and hit his body. Kaintani the kingfisher was back and was hanging out up in his usual roost. Immediately, Anggereai dived into the water. It was just his luck – and he had completely forgotten – that this *bitau* tree was the favourite perch of the kingfisher. The crashing waves on the rock wall and the strong pull of the tide were dangerous. But with the strength of his four sets of legs, Anggereai was able to hold on. That was when he noticed all the shrimp eggs and hatchlings in the gaps between the seaweed.

No wonder so many scavenger fish were loitering there. There was Amumar the moon wrasse, Amperung the crescent perch, and even Kowar, the Whitley's sergeants all bravely dodging back and forth between the stones and the froth of the waves. Their thin bodies tightly hugged the stones, while each fin took a turn in catching the little shrimps and putting them in their mouths. Anggereai was delighted to have found a new food garden. It wasn't until he had filled his stomach that he returned to the surface.

Once he felt full, he rose again to the surface of the water, and immediately looked out for the kingfisher up on the branch. He had positioned himself directly below the perch of the kingfisher, so it was fairly safe. Now, how could he take the water container over to his place? He tried to use a coconut shell as a boat, but it tipped over so easily. He had no choice but to gather some coconut fibre and build a *koisepa* raft. He lifted up the nut that he had filled with water and placed it in the middle. Then he pushed the raft away from the edge of the stone wall and swam, dragging the raft behind. When he arrived at the stone jetty, he dragged the raft into a depression in the stones. Then he brought it closer and lifted the water container onto the rock.

Anggereai was able to do all this with just a little bit of hard work, as he had eight limbs and a set of strong hands to overcome all the difficulties involved. But Andevavait would never be able to do that kind of work. He was certainly clever. But he did not have the physical skills, as he had only two fins and they weren't very strong. Another advantage Anggereai had was his ability to last for days in a dry environment. He was the perfect witness and traveller. His body was thin and emaciated, but not because of under-eating.

Angge, the female crab, hobbled in. Her eyes were red, and her body was trembling. When Anggereai saw her, he put down the water container and went to meet her. She asked in a plaintive voice: 'Where did you get that water?'

'Sorry, I couldn't get water there,' said Anggereai, pointing in the direction of the stream. 'The black ghosts were by the river, so I had to look for it in another place.'

'Black ghosts?'

'If there is smoke billowing, the crows always show up at the fire.'

'So where did you get this water?'

'I found a source of water under the *bitau* tree.'

'Oh, thank you. You're so daring.'

The female took some water to wet the wound on her shell. Then it was Anggereai's turn to help. He kept wetting it over and over again until the female felt her body revive. Anggereai then went back to the stone landing and uncovered the pile of coconut fibre at the bottom of the raft. There were fish eggs and fresh shrimp. He offered the eggs and shrimp, using the coconut fibre as a tray. Without further encouragement Angge tucked in to her fresh repast.

Now that her fever had gone down a bit, she spoke up: 'My dear, thank you so much! You are very kind. But please, I have one request.'

'Request?'

'I feel that the water is not helping much.'

'So what can I do?'

'I think if I do not get some medicinal herbs by tomorrow, the contents of my shell will rot.'

'Oh, if only Andev were here,' said Anggereai.

Without thinking too much ahead, Anggereai quickly guided his female friend back to a recess in the cliff. Then he went back and fetched the water container and put it beside her. He returned to the stone landing and checked out the situation on the beach. The tide was high, and the three people were finally getting ready to leave. The sun was inclining westwards. Anggereai whistled to call Andevavait. Their secret whistle would surely bring him quickly.

# Adventure

Although Raukahi was pampering him at that moment, Andevavait still heard his friend's whistle. It was a call that demanded an immediate response. Andevavait hurried, but before he left he said to Raukahi, 'That's Anggereai calling me – he needs my help. I hope you will stay here. You must wait till I come back.'

Raukahi simply nodded and cautioned him: 'Your body is still weak. You need more rest!'

'Thank you – but I'm fine. I have to get to Anggereai quickly.'

'It's almost dusk, don't be too long.'

Andevavait and Anggereai had no choice but to put off their plans to go into the forest. The path they would take along the river was being watched by a pair of *rawei*, big black crows. Both birds looked extremely vexed as they picked over the bones that still lay scattered around the fireplace. From time to time they made a coughing noise. Perhaps they were upset that they hadn't found whatever it was they were looking for. Perhaps the boy had piled all the leftover bones into the fire. They had hoped for a meal, but there weren't even any scraps left.

Suddenly the two black creatures looked at each other, leapt onto a branch of the *waru* tree and disappeared from sight. Andevavait and Anggereai had been watching them closely and they quickly dived in and swam together across the current. Then all of a sudden Anggereai gave his friend a coded sign to tell him that two people had appeared.

The two men soon came into view, followed by the boy. Oddly, the father's face was beaming. The face of the younger man, on the other hand, looked as if it had been scrubbed with itchy leaves, and his mouth was wide open as if he was begging, desperately seeking a breath of air. His lips were swollen and dripping saliva. It was so strange; he looked as if he had just finished eating chillies without a drink of water. The boy carried a piece of bamboo filled with something. The end of it was sealed with young leaves. Flies were buzzing around the lip of the bamboo.

When they got to the boat the older man put in his machete and then his *noken* bag of *pinang*, areca nuts. Without waiting for the boy, who was dragging the bamboo along the top of the shallow water, the old man began tugging at the boat. The young man joined in to help him drag it across the sand. They stopped for a moment and then continued pulling. Finally the boat reached the edge of the water.

With the high tide arriving so late, Andevavait and Anggereai were not able to do much. They were trapped by their fear of the crows and the villagers. Luckily, now that the boat was in the water, the two friends could continue their journey. But the sun was leaning down in the west; evening would soon arrive. And what if the two black birds were still there, in the shadows of the trees? Darkness was approaching.

Anggereai took the job of watching out for threats from the river bottom and dived into the water, while Andevavait inspected different plants along the edge. But dusk was falling. The plants they were seeking would be difficult to recognize in the dark. Nevertheless Andevavait could rely on his sense of smell. The tide was rising higher, making it easier for their passage in search of healing plants. The closer they got to the lower part of the river, leaving the smell of the mangrove mudflats far behind, the less obvious their path became.

Anggereai was starting to be suspicious of Andevavait, so he left his post watching out for threats that might appear from the river, and joined his friend's search amongst the lines of trees and bushes. Too bad that the rows of mangroves that grew all along the river were covered in darkness here. But the reflection of twilight on the water still lit up the length of the riverbed.

Birdsong greeted them as they entered the estuary. It was a flock of little black *anina* birds that made the most noise. Passing the mangroves with the wide leaves, where they had spent their night, Anggereai and Andevavait were assaulted by the racket. The raucous shouting of thousands of birds hurt their ears so badly that they had to escape under the water. As they approached the mouth of the river the tide was not yet high enough, so they had no choice but to get right down into the mud. There, if just for a moment, they could avoid the high-frequency noise and commotion of the *anina* birds, rarely seen during the day. They flock together in the evening, as the darkness sets in, and at that moment it sounded as if they were celebrating a feast to greet the night. Every now and then flocks of thousands of birds burst free from the mangrove trees and, wheeling like a giant spinning top, a mass of them would circle towards another tree. Then they would return to the original spot, followed by the uninterrupted noise of their deafening cries.

The curious thing about these mangrove dwellers is that they don't make their nests in the mangrove forest. Or even seek their food there. Their nests can be found only in very high trees, deep in the midst of the forest. The *anina* birds weave their nests out of dry grass, cleverly choosing the spot where they make the entry hole, and they nest on the wall of the tree trunk, so it is very difficult for other animals to get at their eggs and baby birds.

They are not at all like the *ampaiso*. These white herons use the dense foliage of the mangrove forest as a place to nest and spend all their lives there. The *ampaiso* usually build their nests in the tips of branches in the densest part of the mangrove swamp. The major threats to their nests are from the eagle and the snake. That's why they always look for food in open spaces, so that they can watch over their nests while they hunt. If a threat appears in the sky they are able return to their nests quickly. To avoid the danger of snakes, their nest has a powerful deterrent – it is made with branches of a special plant that gives off a smell that frightens egg-hunting snakes away.

# Trapped

Night fell at the riverside. Darkness covered the walls of the mangrove forest. Only the silhouette of the sky lit up the glimmering mud terrain. The birdsong fest had been replaced by the sounds of the night.

The rising tide began to flood in around Andevavait and Anggereai. Automatically, they both became very alert, as if they had just woken up from a dream when the muddy surface began to move. Andevavait felt as if a weight was on his body, and so did Anggereai. And now the surface of the mud suddenly seemed to have pores. Some kind of breathing ducts had appeared with the sound of tiny explosions.

From the darkness of the mangrove roots appeared a number of creatures, crawling in their direction. As they came closer, Anggereai gave a sign to Andevavait to be careful. Andevavait understood his friend's concern. The creatures approaching them had a similar body shape to Andevavait. But in this muddy world they looked so much more light and agile: Andevavait and Anggereai found it very difficult to move in the mud. Once they were facing each other they just stayed put, watching. Andevavait tried to communicate with them, but they responded only with angry faces and they started to encircle the two intruders.

Instinctively, Anggereai prepared to protect Andevavait by raising his claws to shield him, but they were surprised to suddenly see a group of crabs appear from behind the mangrove amphibians. These crabs were moving toward the source of the tidal water. Luckily the water had already filled the mud hole, so Anggereai and Andevavait were already finding it easier to move. But this was just the beginning of their adventure in the mangrove forest. So busy was he cleaning mud from his body that Anggereai did not notice one of his legs was sticking into a hole beside the mangrove. The hole closed tight, and Anggereai's leg was trapped by something hard in the mud.

Anggereai jerked away, but it was too late and the vice within the mud tightened. Andevavait cleaned off the mud sticking to his body and prepared to help his friend. But as he approached Anggereai, something else came along with him, dragging behind him through the mud. The hoard of mud creatures that had encircled Anggereai and Andevavait disbanded and moved away, frightened of what was happening. But when an object shaped like a flying saucer poked itself out of the mud, they realized what it was and looked on from a safe distance.

A mangrove mud clam had trapped Anggereai's leg. Ignoring the strength of the strange creature's grip, Anggereai responded by squeezing its lip. Andevavait could do little to help, so he kept cleaning the mud off his body, even as he continued to sink. Soon Anggereai had managed to release himself from the jaws of the clam. The mollusc's shell was extremely thin, so Anggereai was able to pull his leg away. Dragging his leg behind – he felt as if it was paralyzed – he carefully watched out for signs of more traps: they were everywhere.

Anggereai dragged his body along, still sinking in the mud as he moved, all the way to the high-tide pool. There he dived down and allowed himself to stay still in the water. His instinct told him to do this. It was the only thing he could do to help himself. The leg that felt paralyzed was now starting to throb. It was stinging where the mud clam had grabbed him.

Up on the surface Andevavait finished cleaning himself, then he returned to the edge of the mudflat and allowed himself to collapse. He was exhausted; no more struggling across the mud. But he was amazed to see a group of Ambon blennies of his own kind who could move on the mud so lightly and freely, without becoming stuck. Getting out of the mud had taken all his energy. The harder he struggled, the weaker he became. He collapsed and gave himself up to the waves. Then suddenly his body became light.

Discovering a special pleasure in this new lightness, Andevavait began to explore the edges of the water and mud and then the feet of the mangroves. Now fearless, he forgot all about Anggereai and their original plan. Andevavait even forgot about going home. He found a line of holes, then just for fun he started scratching the mud that covered them. Suddenly the mud moved and a giant *aifa* – a karaka crab – appeared and began to chase him. The roots of the mangrove seemed to come alive, and many more *aifa* appeared.

Andevavait found himself trapped in a mudflat by a pile of gravel shaped like a pyramid. The next thing that happened was bizarre. The stones came to life and began to chase him. The shell homes of the *furuhi* – telescopium molluscs or horn snails, those little pyramid-shaped stones – were marching forward, forming lines on the surface of the mud.

Andevavait couldn't turn around. There were lines of karaka crabs following him from behind. Under the reflection of the night sky, the lines and the tracks in the mud looked like there was an army at war, defending the ocean. Andevavait chose to remain still and simply follow the movements of these animals. But no! All those slow-moving creatures were closing in and surrounding him. Then, from the direction of the river mouth, there appeared a school of Ambon blennies. From the shadows around the mangrove trees, threatening crowds of karaka crabs were moving closer. The only chance to escape was to avoid going further upstream.

To stay in this place would be committing suicide. But if he moved he would be chased. He could only wait. The swarm of mosquitoes that had been hovering around his body began to move away. Andevavait could not understand why all the creatures of the mud were scrambling to get close to him.

Perhaps the aroma of salt water that still clung to his body was attracting them? By now the creatures were nearly upon him, so Andevavait dived down and buried his body deep in the mud, completely out of sight. He was safe, but he could barely breathe. He felt the weight of the mud bearing down upon him. The troupe of *furuhi* horn snails had built a heap out of their stony houses on the surface of the mud above him.

# Contemplation

Andevavait could not bear to stay in the mud any longer. Finally, his head emerged, although his body remained sandwiched between the houses of the horn snails. A single *aifa* crab was waiting for him up there, and immediately it pounced upon Andevavait. Andevavait let his body go limp, as if he were dead in the claws of the swamp crab. He felt his waist and his throat being squeezed, but he didn't react. The crab held Andevavait's mud-wrapped body up high, but didn't tear at his flesh. The other members of the karaka pack were now following and they were already arguing over his body.

Suddenly the rowdy ruckus was replaced by the sound of marching feet, distracting the attention of the giant *anggarariti* crabs away from him. The source of the noise came all the way from the river mouth and stopped right in front of the crowd of crabs. Not wishing to be ordered around, the line of karaka crabs spontaneously returned the challenge, raising their claws in the air. The clinch of the claw around Andevavait's body loosened and he slipped out.

He did not waste the chance this offered. For the moment, the karaka was not concerned about his fallen prey. Andevavait's attention had switched to a new threat: from Viwaradi, a giant crested lizard, who was moving steadily towards him, and not even acknowledging the approaching line of giant *anggarariti* crustaceans that continued to wave their pincers in the air.

Andevavait dived as deep as he could, all the way down to the pool of cool, liquid mud at the bottom. He felt the coolness spread throughout his body. The bruises left by the vice of the claws on his waist and his cheek were so sore. He could only stay still. He didn't want to take any more risks. He was wounded and exhausted. There in the mud, which was not his world, he was resigned to his fate. With his eyes tightly closed, only his instinct and his hearing functioned. His cheekbone and its covering of gills was torn. At his midriff the bones felt as if they were broken. After a while, he felt a pool of warm water seeping in from the sea, slowly dissolving the mud that constrained his body. Perhaps after all he still had a chance to return, to go home to his world beside the sea?

Silent in a suspicious space
the goddess of light streams
ten thousand shining rays.
They come raining down
to shatter translucence
circling
converging
in a tranquil eddy.

There is a scream that's seeking silence
There is a road toward the light

..........................
Tired hands, powerless
A piece of roughly etched leaf
with veins like fingers
gives directions to the blue castle.

You who howl
at the foot of the hill,
who used to be so steadfast,
your soldiers are advancing,
the strong ones line the reef.

Some are bleeding
Licking their wounds
The soft ones
dab at dirty faces.
There is a sturdy fist
fiercely scraping a hole.
But you can only curse the lake
where the god is pierced by stakes.

And then,
He becomes a tiger
tearing at his own lies.
He becomes the greatest judge
of his own country's pretenses.

He is the howling
at the base of the hill
The painter of light at the end of the road,
and fire on the face of the sky.


Once he did
sit cross-legged,
his tongue silenced.
Only the air
gathering its flowers.


Within this hazy view
peace was in him like a throbbing pulse.


And once,
He painted a friend
At his side,
'That's my twin from the atoll'
he said.

..........................


The murmur of wind is now howling
as seaweed stretches longingly for the moon
where the eagle rests, in the mangroves
and neither frogs nor jelly-fish know
the tens of thousands of things
that have happened.

But the hawk, who crashes
into the cliff
knows not who will dig his grave.
Who will build up the fire
that burns the mucus
dripping from the cracks
till it becomes as clear as sap
fertilizes roots within the mound
sheds light on the branches
...then on the leaves
...then on the flowers.
and then on the thorns?
Who will be impaled thereon?

..........................

Fodamir, the striped catfish, wounded
The one with the poisonous face
He alone reads the history of the clouds
As written in his library of sand.

He only reads
and reads again.

He only reads
then reads again.

# The Triumvirate of Sound

The moment the high tide reaches the neck of the river and the mangrove dwellers return to rest, it is a sign that the mountain breeze will soon pass by, fulfilling his faithful promise to the ocean. Stunned, Anggereai and Andevavait lay beside a stone and watched the mud arena turn into a lake. They recalled what had just happened to them in that same landscape. Anggereai did not say much. But he wiped tears from his eyes and once he rubbed the leg that had been crushed in the mouth of the mud clam.

Andevavait understood what his friend was going through. He had experienced the same bad luck. And yet after thinking about it, it was actually good luck. If Viwaradi the crested lizard hadn't shown up, he wouldn't be here with his friend. How could Andevavait show his gratefulness to Viwaradi? He didn't know where he came from or where he had gone.

The local people call that time at the beginning of the evening 'afternoon darkness'. By the time the crescent moon appeared in the west, Viwaradi would normally be ready to go to the sea. It was a sign that the mating season had arrived. Although he was not an amphibian, he loved to dive and swim in the water. He had a way of blocking his nose with his forked tongue. If Viwaradi went to the sea, it was not to prey upon fish or to play in the waves. He was called to the ocean for one surprising purpose: to meet his love, Mambara-kamiai the cat shark. Few sea creatures or people know this. Yet the love story of Viwaradi and Mambara-kamiai is one of the strangest and most rare of romantic affairs in the animal world.

It always happened between the coral reef and the edge of the beach. There, Mambara-kamiai and Viwaradi would make love, as if wrestling in the water. What a commotion! It sounded like cats having sex on a tin roof! Sand and mud would scatter in all directions. The surrounding seawater became murky and fish automatically shied away. Despite this odd courtship, once Viwaradi has laid his eggs, from them will emerge a baby *viwaradi*, whereas the eggs in the womb of Mambara-kamiai hatch out into thousands of baby *mambara-kamiai*.

The meaning of the life of a crested lizard begins when his life ends at the hands of the village people. If he is still young when he is caught, then he will be kept and nurtured until his skin is considered ready for use. When his throat is cut, a special mantra must be spoken to request a blessing on the ceremony taking place. His back is then slashed all the way to the base of his tail, and he is skinned. The meat will be eaten, while his skin is placed in the sun to dry. During the skin-drying process, whoever recited the mantra will go to the forest and seek a *marang* tree, source of the special material needed to make Vikainotu, the *tifa* drum.

When he finds the right tree, the mantra-speaker asks it for permission to chop it down. He chants another mantra before starting the felling process. After the tree has fallen, he will seek some special plants in the forest. When he has found them, he will speak, addressing them by a special name, not their real name. Then he will pick several leaves, and place them in his woven *aderi* bag. Once he has dealt with the tree and found the leaves, the mantra-speaker will complete his job by skinning the trunk of the *wainari* tree. This bark has a special sap used for tightening the surface of the skin of Vikainotu the drum.

The leaves, sap and the trunk of the tree – all from living creatures of nature – are carried home by the tree-cutter. Throughout his journey home, whether walking or paddling, that man must continue singing. Today he has been victorious, so he will sing and chant all the way home. He appears to be a solitary man, revelling in his feelings of accomplishment. To some of the villagers, his achievement is seen as an everyday event: he comes home from the forest to the village and applies his skills as a *tifa* drum-maker.

But in the eyes of the older people, his success will be celebrated warmly. The elders do not just welcome the singer as an individual. Instead they speak to him in the plural form, as if he has come home to the village with a crowd of followers. For example, he will be greeted with 'Good afternoon, it seems this afternoon that many accompanied you back in the boat. No wonder your boat appeared so swiftly. Are you planning a feast then?'

The tree-cutter will agree enthusiastically and talk of plans for a feast and dancing, and the time it will take place. He might even announce a *Mandohi*, the special feast for ear piercing, or for payment of a dowry.

When they see the wood that has been cut for Vikainotu in the bow of his boat, the villagers ask him 'Who is that sleeping in the bow of your boat?' The tree-cutter will not reveal his passenger's true identity. Instead he will describe the log as if it were a virgin girl who has just been betrothed to the old man in the roof of the house. By this he means the skin of Viwaradi that is being dried on his roof.

After the wooden log has been hollowed out and decorated with *bui* carving motifs of significance, and the skin of Viwaradi fastened over the opening, then Vikainotu will be considered complete. The tree-cutter tests the drum. A peanut-sized glob of sap from the skin of a *wainari* is stuck on the outer surface of the *tifa* skin. The drum is struck, listened to, and struck again. One by one the sounds are left to echo, while the drum-maker carefully points the face of the *tifa* towards the warmth of his fire embers.

Then the process will be repeated again, to measure the strength of the sound this new companion makes. The essence of the process of creating Vikainotu lies in this collaboration between animal, plant and human to create one meaningful sound. The maker is considered to only facilitate the three-party arrangement, in the creation of his *tifa*. But the face of Vikainotu does not have any meaning without *Mandohi*, the breath of life that is an integral part of the traditions of the people. The presence of this in the drum must be sanctified and celebrated; and Vikainotu will exist in his own right only after an initiation feast has been held. The animals that crawl on the earth, the birds and the plants, all will share in the initiation. Sea-dwellers compare the sounds of such a feast to the variations of the wind on water.

The families of Anggereai and Andevavait are the only

exception. At the time of the feasting they cease all their activities. They must focus upon witnessing and recording. For at the moment when the voice of Vikainotu first reverberates, as he is initiated in the *Mandohi* celebration, all the creatures that walk and all the plants that stir join in arousing the life force incorporated within the *Mandohi*.

# A Tale of Viami

That moment when night falls and the evening choirs become more and more exuberant is the time unearthly guests tend to show up. Only certain elderly people are able to recognize these strangers. They respond instinctively, by singing songs of the world beyond. The women who join in the *Mandohi* start to whisper to each other, and after the final song they hurriedly step aside and gather in the kitchen. Amongst them there are always one or two who have not yet had enough of the dancing – but all they can do is protest. Also, their reluctance is limited to whispering, because it is forbidden to discuss such things with strangers present. They are likely to protest later, when the feast is already crowded. 'Why it is necessary to sing the songs of the spirits?' they ask. But in fact, the singing heralds the climax of the feast. Residents and keepers of the supernatural world and the souls of the ancestors are all expected to attend and join in.

Sometimes strangers appear who do not realize that the elders have lured them there. And in response, those outsiders, who appear both ordinary and ugly, will raise their voices. They cannot be noticed once they join the line of dancing singers. But the vibration of their voices is enough to hypnotize those who hear it. The women amongst them who understand what is happening will quickly gather the girls and disappear with them into a room. The elders will memorize the lyrics that flow from their mouths for later recall.

The conclusion of this gathering occurs when Ampar the morning star appears, a sign that the party will soon be over. That is when the strangers are able return to their homes feeling satisfied. They have attended, persisted and contributed new stories to the elders of the village. Magic tales have been recorded, especially those about the animal world, the world of human beings, even stories about new and unknown things. Perhaps these anecdotes are about things that happened amongst the villagers centuries ago. A transcendent communication has taken form right there, within the *Mandohi*.

Eventually each elder will do his best to remember and store each utterance made by the strangers. When they are alone, to fill the emptiness at moments when freedom fills the soul, especially during the moments approaching dusk, those unseen souls will be in touch with them. Replying in song, the elders will be seen to be enjoying their communication. They look as if they are alone. While they sit on the terrace, on their faces are pictured others that share their feelings.

They go on reciting poetry.

They continue dancing!

Dried leaves of the *wowurai* plants
break from stems and fall in the stream.

A bunch of dead leaves join in the chase
landing easily
then twigs of bamboo
are also shed.

Still the water shows no ripple.
But is that not a cue
to announce the onshore wind?

Pheasant wings beat a warning
Pay attention! Pay attention!

Andevavait, who observed this omen, checked on his friend. Anggereai the crab was completely aloof. Andevavait moved closer and looked right into his eyes. They were unblinking. Andevavait moved his nose closer to the face of his friend. Suddenly a blow hit his ear. Trying to ignore the rush of heat to his ear, Andevavait glared and stuck out his tongue right in front of Anggereai.

'That will teach you not to fall asleep!'

Anggereai exploded. In a single movement he grabbed Andevavait, and gripped his body tightly, as both claws squeezed his friend's neck and cheeks. He felt no resistance: Andevavait was not going to fight back. Embarrassed by what he had done, Anggereai let Andevavait loose, wiping his bleeding cheek.

'It's so sad when friendship turns out like this,' said Andevavait.

Without waiting for a reply, he moved to his original spot at the edge of the stone and looked at the reflection of his damaged cheek in the water. Slowly he washed his wound and examined the side of his cheek that was badly torn. He pushed a slice of cheek that hung from his jaw back into place. Andevavait tried to ignore the pain, but his body trembled and his eyes were full of tears. He was so disappointed by his friend's actions that he could only shake his head.

'My friend, I am so sorry!' Anggereai begged.

Andevavait could see that his friend was sincere, but he felt bitter.

'Never mind. This means I must stay in a dry place until I heal.'

A length of bamboo flashed past and pierced the reflection of his face in the water. Andevavait jerked away. A ripple of water moved out. Amazed, he searched between the trees, but he could see no bamboo growing around the mangrove forest. What kind of sign was this? Looking carefully for the bamboo reflection in the water, Andevavait hastily made a signal to keep away from the edge of the stone. Anggereai understood the sign and checked immediately. A length of upright bamboo in the riverbed turned out to be a swamp snake that was looking for prey. The snake, as big as a piece of *fayamai* bamboo, had been there a while. No wonder there was not a ripple nor the vibration of little fish on the surface of the water. The voice of the frogs, *wiwin-tanggi*, and their occasional responses, sounded earlier as if they were sharing advice: 'Be careful! It's dangerous!'

So that was why the two frogs busking beside the stone

disappeared. Andevavait and Anggereai were right in being suspicious. Fortunately they had already changed their position when the tide was high, and had not neglected to rub mud on their bodies. Now the tide was about to recede. They should quickly get back to the beach, before they were trapped by the low tide. But their main obstacle was still in front of them, and they had not yet found the medicinal herbs. If they did not leave soon, the incident in the mud could be repeated all over again. And what of the fate of the female crab, who was dying? If they put off searching for the herbs until daylight, the risk would be too great to imagine.

# Nature's Forbidden List

There is a sovereign spirit of the sea whose powers cannot be denied. His name is Worri, and he is a sea sprite, greatly feared by village people. He is quick to take offence and he has a terrible temper. He cannot bear his peace to be disturbed. If the light from a boat or a ship so much as passes by within his territory, he will appear with a light of similar brightness and move close to the origin of that disturbing light. This is both a sign and a warning. At any moment the offending boat is likely to hit a coral reef, or reverse the direction of its passage and sail back in the wrong direction.

Worri is just as easily disturbed in the daytime if he detects any strange passing smell – especially the type of smell given off by 'dirty' people who are besmirched by falsity and lies or thievery. He is particularly sensitive to the smell of revenge – bloodstained hands or bodies imbued with lust or the stains of sex. This includes not only the scars left behind by evil things done by people to their own kind, but also from bad things done to any living creature.

On land, for example, there are those who cheat, cut down trees without good reason, or disturb the peace along the river or at the river mouth. In this case Viami – the twin of Worri, who is a land sprite – will spontaneously react. In just a few moments the sky will cloud over and there will be thunder and lightning. In a flash and a roar, rain pours down. Floods appear from the headwaters, picking up piles of rubbish, stones and tree branches on their way. If there is no immediate response, Worri and Viami will together record and memorize the identity of the person responsible, taking special note of the body odour of the offender.

As to division of their realms of power – as the guardian of the sea, Worri is connected to the water while Viami, guardian of the land, always flies around and hangs out with the wind. The wind and the water are like an extension of their senses, as well being as their means of communication. The peace will be disturbed if either wind or water becomes polluted. Not polluted by artificial, dirty, material rubbish, as viewed through the eyes of people, but rather that kind of pollution that results from the actions of those who behave indiscriminately toward their fellow creatures. And within the being of each living creature, especially humans, also dwells a medium with a high potential for absorbing the interactions between Worri and Viami, depending upon the location and the conditions at the time.

Worri and Viami are twins entrusted with ensuring harmony of dialogue among all living creatures. This balance will be maintained if each living creature fulfils his responsibility as expected. And humans, as creatures who live by understanding others, constantly giving birth to new leaps of civilization, must always sustain their tolerance for other creatures in order to keep the harmony among all. The peace between Worri and Viami will be disturbed if any connection between the two is contaminated.

When human civilization pulls down the boundaries between Worri and Viami, knowledge about them is displaced and piles up – within individual and collective, shared territories. It is the body odour, linked to ancestry as it is passed on through generations, that bears evidence of an accumulation of such imbalance.

Worri and Viami will never expire; their powers will never end. Just as the water and the wind will continue to flow and blow until everything is piled up at one end; it banks up like notes and files until it forms a mountain. From then on it will be a matter of waiting to find out in what direction the piles of wind and water must spill over. The only thing certain is that in the end everything must return to balance, as in the past.

Everything must find a state of harmony.

# The Benefactor

Bohurai the toadfish, understanding the friendship of Andevavait and Anggereai, always tried to nurture their relationship. On the other hand, he wondered how he could ensure that these two friends would not discover his secrets. At the same time he must commit to his personal agreement with Andevavait, so that he could still be seen as learning to fast. Whenever he was in view on the surface, Bohurai continued fasting. But what happens on the surface is not always the same as what happens underwater.

As in the beginning of the story, Andevavait the tidepool blenny had trusted Bohurai the toadfish to safely round up the fruit of the coconut palm dropped from above. But at the time it couldn't all be gathered securely. Bohurai had no way to prove that two bunches of coconuts had either sunk or had been carried away by the current. That was why Anggereai and Andevavait secretly suspected him and watched Bohurai's behaviour so closely. They understood the dire consequence of losing two bunches of coconuts – the ritual of bamboo cutting had already been carried out. True, Andevavait was the perpetrator and ready to accept the outcome. But after thinking about it and calculating, he felt sure that the keeper of stolen goods should be more severely punished. Would the sacred ritual of cutting bamboo take its toll, and could it affect creatures other than human beings?

Upon observation it seemed that a change was taking place in Bohurai's behaviour. Even while he was fasting, the toadfish often held feasts to share his 'good luck'. Evidence of this could be seen as scavengers frequently gathered at Bohurai's dwelling. Just before sunrise Bohurai would share fatty tidbits with them. So much that toadfish was now known as a kind benefactor. Maybe this was a result of his fasting.

The question was, where did he get the fatty treats that they were sharing? It was quite clear that the toadfish now had an increasingly large stomach, and he spent all his time sleeping. Moreover, there were ever more scavenger fish hanging around him. Some of the underwater creatures did not care in the least about Bohurai. But Andevavait and Anggereai felt that the time would soon come when they could prove what Bohurai was up to.

According to the latest news from Anggereai, it was said that the siblings of Bohurai – Borotha and Boanshina – often visited and took their share of the spoils as well.

# A Quiet Moment

The canoe docked next to some steps made from a tree branch that had been propped up against the balcony at the front of a stilt-house. There were only two houses here and they were located at the furthest outpost of the village, some distance from the dozens of other houses with tin and sago-leaf roofs, their walls made of sago branches. One side of the house looked out towards the road and was connected by a gangplank to a small wooden bridge. When night arrived, the gangplank would be pushed to one side, to make it impassable for others, especially unwanted guests.

The woman who had slumped in the bow of the canoe weakly pulled herself up and crawled into the house. The children who awaited her, all lined up along the edge of the upper level, could see by her face that there was something wrong. They followed her in. Usually they would jostle for a good position at the edge of the balcony to welcome their parents. If the canoe had been loaded with the fruits of their catch, they would have scrambled to fight over the best fish or shellfish, and it wouldn't be long before smoke would be seen billowing from the roof of the kitchen. But this time the children had no choice but to resist their longing; they could not protest. This was a house in which children were forbidden to argue back. Protesting to a parent was taboo, and in the ancestral home this rule still carried weight. Here Rawei would not allow any compromise, especially with his own offspring; it was necessary in respect for the longhouse.

Wondi Rawei, that was his full name. Those on familiar terms called him Rawei, after the black crow. He was the faithful guardian and gatekeeper of his ancestors' traditions. Very extreme in his ideals, he refused to compromise with new values. He had his own way of challenging the modern education at the village school; he instructed his children in the all the ways of the ancestors. According to him, the new values that had been introduced by the foreigners should not be followed in his village. In reality it could not be like that. Even the ancient teachings could no longer fully answer all the problems that entangled their lives. And now religion completely forbade all traditional rituals. But when a tsunami hit their village, all the houses were destroyed except for the Wondi family longhouse.

After that, many villagers rushed to leave the ruins of the old village and they built a new kampong, closer to the mainland. They thought the site of the old village was a haunted place and it was shunned. Moreover at the new village a number of longhouses were dedicated as places of worship. At first Rawei thought the families of the same bloodline would live in those long houses, as with the ancestral house of the Wondi family. He was wrong. Rawei, his roots firmly planted within the ancestral Wondi family, then built his own house alongside the existing one. Only three persons lived in this longhouse: Grandma Wo and the youngest, Mando. Living with them was a short-legged woman whose behaviour had never grown past childhood even though she was as old as Rawei. This tiny woman still remained a faithful retainer and companion, looking after Grandma Wo.

One day a family of white people arrived in the kampong, and settled into one of the priest's houses. There was a husband and wife, and two girls. Every day the white couple was seen busily carrying notebooks from house to house in the village. The two daughters were left to play with the village girls. They were very friendly and kind to the inhabitants. At every chance to chat, they always wrote down the meanings of the words and the wise sayings that were contained within them. They made no exception of the two secluded houses at the far end of the kampong: the longhouse of the Wondi family and the Rawei family in their sago-branch house. The white couple made no visits on Sundays. On that day they joined in to worship at the church, after which they returned to the house of the priest and continued reading and writing.

At the beginning of their visit to the sago-branch house, the Rawei family were very nervous and suspicious. The wife was especially afraid that her husband, who always returned home in the evening, would find the white couple there. But she appreciated the gentleness of the white woman, who never hesitated to keep her company, joining her in her smoky kitchen, so eventually her suspicions evaporated. When she told her husband of their visits, Rawei had nothing to say. His forehead creased slightly, then he returned his focus to his daily work routine, preparing the fishing hooks and lures, then disappearing back into his room. Not long after that, the sound of betel nut being pounded in his *airokung* could be heard from behind the sago-branch walls.

One Sunday afternoon the white man arrived unexpectedly at the house of Grandma Wo. Mando's canoe was tethered to the pole in front of the house. The two dogs that usually greeted the white man with wagging tails were nowhere to be seen. He called out a courteous greeting. Nobody replied. Then he called out the name of the 'tiny one', addressing her politely as 'mother'. The bent body of Grandma Wo suddenly appeared to unfold at the front door as she rose up to greet the white man. Grandma Wo then crooned a little tune, as if coaxing a child onto her knee, first asking the white man in, then in the same breath continuing to complain about her companion who was late in returning from her bath. Without giving the white man a chance to reply, Grandma Wo then asked him why his wife was not with him. Patiently the white man waited for her stop talking.

Slowly and slightly stammering in his effort to choose suitable words, the tall American man outlined his reasons for not bringing his wife along. Grandmother Wo was delighted to hear her mother tongue spoken so perfectly; pride shone from her wrinkled but tranquil features.

Then the American said, 'I noticed a canoe moored in front of the house. Perhaps the owner of the canoe had just returned from the sea?'

Suddenly the face of the grandmother became serious. 'Don't ask me about that again.' They were quiet for a moment, then Grandma Wo's expression relaxed. 'My youngest, Mando, and his brother next door never go out to sea on Sundays.' She said that they had been observing this abstinence ever since the time of their ancestors. Long before people knew about praying in the church.

She noticed the expression of the white man was becoming

more and more serious as he listened to her. Rawei's mother went on to explain that on days of rest such as that day, it was not permitted to carry out any activities, except in the kitchen. Even those activities should be carried out without any rowdy noise or babble at all, as it could disturb the others who were resting in their rooms. In principle, that day was regarded as a time for silence.

Then Grandma Wo told the American that their conversation was being overheard by Mando on the other side of the wall. The American seemed surprised to hear this from the grandmother, but she only smiled, understanding how easily confused the white man must be. At that moment the 'tiny one' appeared back from the waterfall, followed by her two escorts, and bearing a couple of lengths of bamboo filled with water. When they passed the front porch on their way to the kitchen, the white man noticed how nimble she was; she didn't make the slightest noise.

The American was about to leave when he saw Mando standing in the doorway. This must be the one Grandma Wo had warned him was listening in to their conversation.

Without further ado, Mando directly told the white man how much he admired his ability to speak their language. But from whom had he learned it? The white man saw his opportunity. Glancing aside at Grandma Wo, he said, 'The one who taught me was your own mother. And all the other villagers have helped.'

The young man exclaimed in surprise. He thought a moment and then remarked that it was less than a year ago that the white man and his family had arrived in the kampong, and up until now they had never met.

'But how, in this short time, are you already able to speak our language? Perhaps you used Antarawihi?'

The man asked him, 'What is Antarawihi?'

'So there is something that you have not yet written about in your book after all.'

Grandma Wo quickly took the white man's side. 'This sort of thing isn't possible to discuss with a priest,' she said, 'and the villagers could not possibly have told them about it.'

But Mando reasoned that those leaves of knowledge were for neither Viami nor Worri. 'The priest must be afraid to talk of them. Antarawihi is the magic leaf. It holds the key to all knowledge since the creation of our ancestors. Even before animals and people existed on the earth, the creator had left it for us, among the plants and the trees. Only the purest of people could take and use it.'

The white man felt that he was starting to understand. 'The clever leaf was the big book from our Lord Jesus,' he said.

'What leaves did your Lord Jesus teach you to read?' said Mando.

'The teachings are in the big book,' the American replied.

'So who is this Lord Jesus?'

'Jesus was sent by his father in heaven,' said the American.

'If that's true, can you speak the name of the father of Lord Jesus out loud?' said Mando.

At this, the white man paused and pondered. Then he replied in the language of Grandma Wo. Mando asked him where he had got those words.

'From the priest, and your mother told me they were true,'

he replied.

'Oh I see. Could you explain it to me more clearly then? Those people who go to church often say their Lord Jesus likes to go net fishing in the ocean. If that is so, your Lord Jesus surely teaches you all the names of the fish. Can you tell me the names of the fish under the sea?'

The white man remained silent. It was hard to know where to start explaining something rational to a person like Mando.

Then he said, 'To master knowledge so that we can speak another language quickly, it is necessary to study. That is why in my country children are sent to school from a young age, and the learning continues till they are adults, even right up until they are old.'

The white man explained that even now, he and his wife were still studying their own language. They wrote things down, so they wouldn't forget them. From the time they were very young, they were used to studying, writing things down and then reading over what was written. They repeated this process until they had it firmly saved in their heads.

Now it was the turn of Mando to remain silent.

Then the white man excused himself to Grandma Wo, and Mando escorted him to the gangplank. When they arrived at the end of the bridge, the young man spoke to him again.

'When you go back to your country, don't forget to teach our language to the children at your school there, because our schools do not wish to teach our own language to the children,' he said. 'Here, they consider our own language old-fashioned and out of date.'

# Mangga-maraing and the Boiling Water

The sky was burning on the horizon. At the beginning of the morning, the face of the water looked like oily blood. A flock of seagulls were crossing on their way to Airing, in the region known as Air Mendidih, or 'boiling water'. There they would race with the Mangga-maraing fishermen. Those fishermen who preferred to paddle were waiting. They caught fish by paddling fast and trailing a lure and hook at a particular distance behind them.

The bait was a lure made from chicken feathers attached to a hook. This lure must be tugged at intervals, so it moved amongst the tiny anchovy-like fish in time with the surge of the hand and the rhythm of the paddler. But the contest between the seagulls and the fisherman was not an attempt to outdo each other, but for both sides to seek rewards.

Those anchovies that made the water boil were driven to the surface by the tuna who hunted them. The lure was camouflaged to look like one of them, so that it would be sought in turn by the tuna. These are the moments when the seagulls take their share. The seagulls fly and twist, following the movement of the school of tiny fish, occasionally diving down to pounce. Then they fly again. Even after they have eaten their fill they keep following the direction of the current and the fish. Like the tuna that are already satiated, they too eventually disappear into the seascape. The Mangga-maraing will be left behind counting the results of their hunt on one side of the boiling water. After disappearing for a few minutes, the bubbling water will appear in another spot. And so it is that the seagulls and the Mangga-maraing fishermen compete to start the next session.

The bubbling water caused by the regular activity of these living creatures, just like the anchovies, will go on moving forever from place to place. However at Airing's Air Mendidih, the place where the Mangga-maraing tribe choose to spend their lives, there is a different reason for the activity in the water. This is because here there is gas bubbling out of the bowels of the earth that makes the water appear to boil. The ancestors treated this place with great respect and considered it to be sacred. Airing was thought to be a blessing and a source of fish from the gods, who would take care of them and their descendants. Accordingly, they always protected Airing, so that it would never be entered, nor its yield ransacked by the fishermen from another kampong.

But today the Mangga-maraing people are facing a different challenge, because it turns out that Airing is a source of mineral gases. And the progress of technology in their home country has not been limited just to outboard motors. There, technology has already reached outer space and is monitoring them as they fish at Air Mendidih. They could now control only the surface of the water. Meanwhile minerals are being extracted, and they are distributed across the base of the earth. They pervade the sea, the islands and villages, all the way to the traditional territories of the most foreign tribes on the land. The local people are allowed to watch over the surface of the water at Airing, but modern technology has the capacity to suck the source dry, from a place far away from their traditional territory.

# Amidst a Thousand Islands

Dreams come true
on a single Island.

Paddle between islands,
trace the peaceful coast
There is only the sound of a paddle
tap-tap-tapping on the wooden hull,
Counting out loud, one by one,
down one side of the island.

One by one, the trees are counted,
One, two, the leaves remembered,
Altogether, the bushes greeted
One-two, friends safeguarded.

At the end of the island
Wanamba the east wind challenges.
And the struggle continues,
measuring the opposite shore,
he casts his line, stalking hope
upon this blue horizon;
even the edge has an end.

Rounding Marirori the calm coast
to the lilt of the north wind Wanampui,
blowing its tune, breath of the mainland,
singing with the paddle's tap on the hull.


Oily mirror on water's face,
counting corals, one by one,
reading names, one, two.
In time the face is carved.


Gliding on Marirori's calm sea
carving a groove
in the mirror-like face
sought by the sea-snake.

Beware of reflections in the water
pray the seaweed is untangled
where Wohe and Mori dwell,
spirit guardians of the land and air
Mamboasar the seahorse
is tempted by Mantemboni seaweed fruits.


The *kambuwir* spear stays still
even Nuai is silent

The lion-fish puffs his chest
As the bird of paradise daydreams.

Flames burn
them together
with their dreams.

The jellyfish blushes red,
his fingers spread wide
as he invites suitors
with a soft caress.

Rohai, the gravedigger shrimp and
Sera-mambiti the Gobyfish stand guard,
caretakers of the sweet Manumggarum seaweed
their hidden store of food.

Heading for Marirori
reading the pool between the islands.
Perfect as a well-cast net
Munua's song goes round
as thousands of fish are caught at once;
count the catch so there's none left over.

Sharing evenly
the same in the bow
Sharing half,
the same again in the tub
even the stern is full.

Exact same shares divided,
to be enjoyed equally by all.

# The Early Feast

During their days of old age, towards the end of their lives, Anggereai and his wife invited Andevavait to dinner. After eating together, they drew out the evening by drinking the palm toddy, *je vereng*, as they waited and prepared to greet their maker.

As the host, Anggereai prepared three bowls made from shells of the *matoa* seed. He filled all three bowls equally, then without waiting, Anggereai drank down his entire portion, put the bowl back down and waited for a few moments. Anggereai's wife and Andevavait looked at each other. Anggereai understood what was in their minds.

'It doesn't have poison in it,' he said. 'Please drink!'

After emptying his *matoa* shell, Andevavait said to Anggereai, 'My friend, you never told us about this beverage.'

'It is a drink that belongs only to the people of this village.'

'Did you take it from the village then? How did you get it?'

'It was a gift from Bapa Adé Mando. Bapa Adé was drunk and had fallen asleep on the beach. Rather than let it all tip out, I saved what was left over.'

'How did you do that?'

'At the time, Bapa 'dé Mando was paddling alone. That

morning it was high tide, so his canoe could slide right into the river and follow it all the way into the mangrove forest. By the time he came back the tide was out – "*Meti siang*". Pa' dé Mando's canoe was high and dry near the mouth of the river. While he waited for the tide to come in, he made a fire at the edge of the river and grilled a couple of flat-tailed longtoms, the ones we call *ansanai-moya*.'

'Who is this Bapa Adé Mando?' asked Andevavait.

'That's young Pa-che, the one who collects the *je anggadi*!'

'Ooh …! Pa-che, that one who is always getting drunk?'

'*Ya*, that's him! My wife says the villagers call him Pa' dé Mando. That name has several meanings.'

'Could it come from the word *mandohai* or … *Mandohi*?'

Anggereai had forgotten and he asked his wife to correct him.

'It could also be from *mandoni* or perhaps even from the word "*mandong*" – the seaweed we use to make our fishing nets,' she said.

'That's right, thank you,' said Anggereai. Then he turned to his guest. 'Andev, have another drink.'

Andevavait pushed a cup toward Anggereai.

Pouring *je vereng* into the cup, Anggereai continued.

'My friend! Actually, our reason for inviting you is that we have one last wish. We know you have many tales to tell about the world of man. Perhaps you still have a good story tucked away somewhere? Surely you will share that story with us!'

'Sorry, but I only know a little,' said Andevavait. 'As far as I remember, people sometimes compare their lives with the outside world, including our world.'

Andevavait picked up his bowl, and so did Anggereai and his wife. Anggereai's wife told a story about the warriors from the village, a story that ended tragically. Then she told a story about the war to capture slaves between one village and another, and then she burst into song, and sang a song about that story.

Towards the end, Anggereai stopped his wife: 'Hey, wait! I know that song!'

'Who do you know it from?' said his wife.

'I just think I've heard it somewhere.'

Anggereai and Andevavait looked at each other and smiled. The female crab was confused. She looked at them both and said, 'If you know the song, why don't you sing it?'

Anggereai and Andevavait looked at each other again. Anggereai searched for the right note and sang the song from the beginning. Andevavait responded in typical drunken style.

Shape-shifters
Where does this road lead?
It seems to go so far
Like the depths of the ocean, no one can guess
but we are wandering around the house
walking in circles, confused.
This is who we are, village shape-shifters.

This road leads so far
for a duty so heavy
sinking to the depths of the sea, unmeasured
here and there, all our lives.

Filling our days.
This is who we are, village shape-shifters.

This road leads so far
for a duty so heavy
sinking to the depths of the sea, unmeasured
here and there, immersed in life
filling our days
by the lagoon.

*(\* See Original Ambai song on P.206.)*

When the song was over, the female crab protested: 'Why does it have to be in such a drunken style?'

Anggereai smiled at his wife's comment and, picking up his bowl, he started to sing the song again, but his wife rushed to stop him.

'Now you must tell me, where did you hear that song!'

He replied by singing another song.

# Prince of the Sun

O Prince of the Sun
Your face so cold and harsh
Your fangs, a pair of tusks
yellow-brown,
curving beneath your chin.
Your skin, speckled black
hair long and greying
to match your flapping silver cloak.
You ride an orange chariot
Pulled by twelve thousand flying fish
that emerge from the sea
to follow the path of the sun.
And the chariot stops
alongside the crown of Anggereai.
O Prince of the Sun
Step inside
Find your inner being.
Within you
dwells a selfless soul
that moves restlessly.
Then you will be carried away,
toward the eastern sun.
While waiting there
in the darkness of night

you paint the stars,
counting them one by one.
Where the sun rises
you too will rise.
Then the Prince of the Sun
leaves his orange chariot
as it passes on
through the wind's thousand colours.

All that remains is yellow dust
on the shoulder of the hill.

# We-dobarai: the Last Party

*We-dobarai!* Thunder rumbled from an approaching storm.

A roaring rainstorm had just struck the edge of the beach. Flashes of lightning tore at the darkness of the night, breaking the silence of the sleeping creatures on land and the cave dwellers at the bottom of the ocean.

Andevavait, the guest of Anggereai and his wife, had no choice but to spend the night at their place. After dinner, Anggereai took Andevavait aside, and together they entered the food store, where Andevavait was amazed to see a stock of drinks in a row of bamboo containers. His friend encouraged him to try some, and then without thinking twice, he kept on drinking.

Soon he was very drunk, and Andevavait began to reveal his innermost feelings regarding Raukahi the octopus, how much he missed him and what a loss his departure had been. That night he vented all his pent-up feelings. It was already several full moons ago that he had split up with Raukahi. As he drank the *je vereng* toddy, Andevavait imagined Raukahi having a bath. What a beautiful sight it was. Perhaps Raukahi was a nymph that had been transformed into an octopus? Bathing nude and dancing, his body seemed to dissolve, and all that remained was a reflected image of seven dancers.

Now Andevavait began to dance. Anggereai exploded with laughter. Andevavait paused to see what he was laughing at, but Anggereai couldn't stop laughing. Andevavait decided he didn't care and kept on dancing his drunken dance, releasing all his feelings of longing. It seemed as if Raukahi was actually there with him, and he kept dancing until he was too tired to go on and he fell asleep.

The following day, when he woke up he found Anggereai sitting beside him, offering him breakfast.

'My friend, where is the Sleepy Village?' Andevavait said, while enjoying the food. 'You know, the garden where they make the drink?'

'The garden?' replied Anggereai. 'That's a long story!' He smiled as he recalled Andevavait's behaviour the night before.

'What's the matter? Is something funny?'

'Never mind. I was just remembering your dancing last night.'

'You are poisonous! Enough!'

Andevavait put down his breakfast and got up as if to leave, but Anggereai hurriedly stopped him.

'What's the matter, friend? Are you angry?'

'It's nothing. I just want to go and have a pee.'

'Oh, be careful. I thought must want to dance some more.'

'That stuff made me feel very good,' said Andevavait.

When he headed for the back room Andevavait passed Anggereai's wife who had just arisen from her sleep. How surprised he was at what he saw: she looked haggard and old. When he returned to meet Anggereai, Andevavait wanted to ask his friend about Angge's strange transformation. But he resisted the urge. He was afraid of offending Anggereai. After breakfast, Andevavait directly excused himself and returned home.

Outside, the sun had just appeared at the end of the cape.

Sunlight was evaporating the dew on the wet brown granite stones of the cliffs. The luxuriant leaves of the *bitau* tree trembled, anxious for the warmth of the sun. Now the sea was calm; it looked as if nothing had happened the night before.

But the white sand beach was full of rubbish from the ocean floor. Moss and seaweed, empty seashells and dead jellyfish had been cast up and were piled all along the beach. Such is the caprice of nature; no humans can prevent it from happening. The elders in the village believe that whenever a natural disaster like this takes place, there will be a sacrifice. Either that or something important is about to take place.

Andevavait changed his plans. He would not go home. He decided to stay on at Anggereai's, the place where he and Anggereai usually kept an eye on their surroundings. But his thoughts kept coming back to what he'd seen in Anggereai's kitchen. Strange: it was as if a third person stayed with Anggereai and his wife. If she was Anggereai's wife, why was her face so old and wrinkled? Or maybe Angge's grandmother stayed with them. But if that was the case, then why, after all this time, had he never been introduced?

The sun was rising higher, spreading light over the surface of the water. The light flared in reflection, blocking Andevavait's view of something that was bobbing in the tide. It was getting closer to the stone where he had spent his time fasting. But there was another reflection beckoning to him, calling him from the beach.

Ignoring the call from the beach, Andevavait quickly dived in to check what it was that he had seen.

The empty shell of a *konggomirai* mollusc was stuck on the edge of the stone. Andevavait dragged the shell-boat closer to the flat part of the stone and checked its contents. There he saw a baby octopus squirming at its exposure to the sunlight. He could hardly believe what he saw.

Then he suddenly remembered Raukahi. Immediately he looked all around, and then he dived under to see below, but he could not find any trace of his friend. He went back up to look at the baby octopus. Without thinking any further, he took the baby and put it in the cave. He left it in a small ditch that had filled up with water. This pool would not be affected by the high or low tide, unless the coral was overturned.

Feeling that in this place the baby octopus would be safe, Andevavait quickly went back to search around the area. Who knows, he might find the baby's mother. There was no sign of her. Nonetheless, Andevavait felt happy, for now he had a new friend, even if his new friend was still a baby. Especially since Raukahi had left him without any message, except for that strange shield.

He tried to forget his past misunderstanding with Raukahi, but one thought kept bothering him. What if that thing left behind by Raukahi was some kind of message? Hurriedly Andevavait went to pick up the keepsake, the puzzling eight-sided shield that Raukahi had left him, saying only, 'Keep this, and one day you will find your soul mate.'

Andevavait put the eight-sided shield away and then hurried to check for calls from the beach. The reflections had already disappeared. But he still remembered the spot where the refracted light had come from on shore.

His sense of curiosity continued to draw him closer to the beach. First, though, as was customary before setting out on an adventure away from his base, he needed to know what dangers might be lurking outside. Primarily he needed to check where Kaintani the kingfisher was. There was no sign of him on the branch of the *bitau* tree. The beach was still covered in wreckage and mess. A fishy smell had begun to cover the entire strand, attracting scavengers from the land such as *bilolo* lizards, giant ants and beach herons, as well as rats and porcupines. They were all seeking their share, scavenging for a bit of the luck that had been vomited out of the stomach of the ocean. Then Andevavait heard a short whistle, a signal from a friend. Anggereai appeared. He, too, was watching what was unfolding on the beach.

For nearly an entire day, the two of them watched the free feast as it took place all along the beach. The two friends diligently observed everything that happened, one event at a time. Umahi, from the line of *bilolo*, who was camouflaged to look like grains of sand, carved a picture of fish on the beach. Fiawera the bush dog was the first to leave his mark, just as the feast began. Only the wild pig and Mansoari the cassowary could not be seen. All the other forest dwellers on the giant island were present at the feast and mingling together.

In the distance, up in the young branches of the *kadoi* beach almond tree, they saw the shape of Fimuna the slow loris. He was looking both shy and amazed as he watched the feasting on the carrion of sea creatures. He preferred to be lazy and only once had he ever joined in this kind of affair. This free-for-all feasting on the beach was not something that he wished to be a part of; he understood he was destined to be a lazybones, an eater of plants and fruit. Anyway, nature had scheduled a season for him to pick what he needed, and that was enough. But he still recorded this incident of the ocean having thrown up everything inside. He memorized every detail he saw, along with all the changes that took place.

But if Fimuna was caught for some feast in the village, he could only accept his fate. It is rare to see his tears, but when he cried the vibrations of sadness could be heard echoing the entire length of the mountain slopes. Then every fruit-eater would be aghast and raise the alert. None would dare to take any action. When the smoke billowed forth from the kampong, the sea breezes would carry the scent of their friend's demise and the aroma of his heart roasting could be smelled all the way up to the mountain. Torn with grief, they would mourn together, openly.

Together those creatures would give thanks for their survival, sending off one great prayer in unison, so that each fruit-eater could continue his activities with pride. It was they who gave the jungle its breath.

In spite of its high cost, the skin of Fimuna the slow loris is the most undervalued thing in the world of mankind. Nonetheless, the highest position in Paradise is reserved for him.

# A Legacy of Pearls

That night, after working all day catching little shrimps and moving them into the ditch, Andevavait took a rest and watched over the baby octopus, who seemed to be starting to enjoy playing with the little creatures. Andevavait was amazed that he didn't hunt them and capture them. Or maybe the baby octopus wasn't hungry yet? He watched him stretch out his tentacle, while the baby shrimps twirled about it, then the little legs tested the adhesive dots on the baby octopus's digits. The bodies of the tiny shrimps jerked in surprise, as if there was an electric current on the tentacles. Andevavait was fascinated at the way these little creatures were getting to know each other. They played their game over and over, and they seemed to be getting more and more familiar.

Then Andevavait began to realize, in the night of the dark room, that the hole in the stone was very bright, as if in broad daylight. Not able to believe his eyes, Andevavait moved out and realized that outside it was actually dark. The stars were scattered over the sky. So why was it so bright inside the cave? He hurried back in and stopped in the doorway to the cave. Slowly his eyes sought the origin of the light, and there it was, in the corner, where he had placed the shield left behind by Raukahi. The shield was the source of light.

He moved closer to the thing. The silvery grains that he had thought were beads were giving off an incandescent glow. Why had this not happened during daytime? Apparently those things that he had thought were beads had no holes in them, and the conglomeration in the shape of a shield was made up of many, all stuck to each other to form eight sides.

Andevavait put the glowing shield down, and then looked carefully back at the reflection of the light on the stone walls. Perhaps Raukahi had left it to light up his life?

He thought back over the path of his life up to the time he had met Raukahi, and the moment that they had been forced to split – for the sole reason that they had to each follow their own destiny, because they were different creatures. At the time of their last meeting, he had thought Raukahi had lost a tentacle as a result of making a deal with Andawai to dig the hole for him to dwell in. But it turned out that the main cause was humans acting with no concern for the world. Actually, as water creatures, just as with many other types of fish, they should have understood each other's nature. There were only two duties in this life: survival – to be sacrificed in the end by fellow fish in their own sea world; or, even more noble: sacrifice – when a life ends in dedication to the survival of mankind.

In the end Raukahi had to lose that other tentacle. It was truly tragic, the fate of the octopus. Andevavait remembered when they parted, how Raukahi had counted and chosen to sacrifice one of his seven remaining digits. All of them had the same value and function. To choose the tentacle in line with the stump, or another, that was the question. So that it would not look too odd, in the end the choice fell to the fourth digit, counting from the stump, so that between each stump there would be three tentacles that remained intact. Raukahi would have to wait a very long time for the tentacles to grow back. And he knew exactly what this would mean. It was only now that Andevavait realized that Raukahi had actually promised he would not show himself again after he had sacrificed his tentacle.

Never mind: Raukahi was living his own life now. But if this baby octopus was his, why had he left it all alone to drown? And what of the fate of Konggomirai who had provided the shell house he had used as a boat?

Certainly, a shellfish that lost his house would become a sacrifice to the continuation of another creature's life. Now he recalled the ray of warning light that had bounced back from the beach. Andevavait headed back out and decided to cross to the beach in a rush.

Andevavait dived into the water and swam in the direction of the beach. But he could hear a buzzing sound following him from behind.

Oh dear, he thought, his movement in the water must be so easy to see – sparks of florescent light were pulsing in the water around him and brightening his path. Spontaneously he changed his position, rising toward the surface of the water. Just then a predator swept down upon him. He jumped, together with an *ansanai-moyang* fish that was also dodging the attack; and Andevavait got away. He gathered all his energy and his body seemed to soar like a Wofai flying fish. Finally the wave breaking on the beach carried him ashore and cast him onto the sand.

Andevavait remembered the position of the pile of rubbish that he had marked. But the situation on the beach had changed completely in the past few days. Some of the rubbish had been swept away by waves, and it was only on the higher part of the beach that the remains of the old rubbish could be seen. On this part of the beach he could still smell something dead. Andevavait marked the position with a branch that had fallen and leaned on the roots of the *kawawori*, a kind of beach pandan tree.

There were several sources of flashing light at the time – he remembered they came from the same direction. It was difficult to move on the dry sand, but Andevavait managed to get to the end of the fallen tree. From here on it was easier. The *biawak* lizard Kamantifu had over-eaten and was moving away from the fallen trunk. His stomach was so bloated that he could hardly move across the dry sand.

'You greedy ...' Andevavait started to curse him. It seemed that the free spoils vomited from the sea had in the past few days made all the creatures alike: after over-stuffing themselves they were now too lazy to move far.

Stopping at the place he had marked, he was smitten by the dreadful smell of a corpse. 'There must be dead bodies here somewhere,' he thought, 'but what kind of creatures could they be?'

He moved closer to the end of the log, but he saw nothing suspicious. A pile of brown *vakihing* seaweed and green and white *vavuta* seaweed had dried up and was spread out over the sand. He saw a line of red ants strung out along the length of the tree. He didn't want to go any further. Better to think about his return journey, planning carefully how to avoid danger, as he had on his way here. Certainly he would not follow the same track. He must hug the edge of the coast, then move to the end of the beach which was shaded by coconut palms; from there it would be closer and safer. The situation on the beach was not so frightening after all. Now he felt calmer. Because of the great abundance of food from the ocean, all the land creatures seemed to have eaten their fill.

Andevavait heard the voice of thunder in the distance. He tried to stay still and looked straight ahead without blinking. There was a streak of light at the end of the rainbow, a sign that there would be a storm. With that in mind, he looked around closer at hand. He saw two groups of ants disappearing in two lines under the green and white *vavuta* seaweed. Then the droves of ants reappeared. Those carrying food passed it to the new arrivals on their way out.

The smell of death was still stinging his nostrils. Then he realized where it was coming from, for in the midst of the dry seaweed there shone a thin ray of light. Ignoring the rotten smell, Andevavait leapt back onto the sand and spun back around in the direction of the waves.

Andevavait had been holding his breath too tightly for too long. He let it explode out until his lungs were empty. His body felt weak, and he lay as still as a statue. Evidently, this was where the shield with its lights must have come from. Two pearls lit up the night as the group of ants worked. They wallowed between the two points of light squeezed inside the shell of Sawerarai the mollusc. His was the thinnest shell of all the molluscs, and it was as wide as a sea-hibiscus leaf. His body looked as if it was broken and rotting. But his shell house was still intact. The muscle holding both sides of the shell was smashed and also decomposing, and Sawerarai's usually tightly clenched mouth had sagged open, leaving just enough space for the parties of ants to enter. Even Anggereai's thin body would find it difficult to get into that cavity, let alone Andevavait.

Suddenly a single spiky Manggairawa lizard ran across the sand, distracting Andevavait. Just then he heard the sound of a thunderstorm approaching from the sea. Andevavait had no choice but to turn back – he had to get away from there.

# O Butterfly

Kamambo...
My darling butterfly so long awaited
you stopped by at last.

Noon refuses to budge.
the stone jetty
trampled by bare feet
of village children
spirits gleeful
in poetry
raiding the foam
when Tobura the Conch shell echoes
If only....
she would come and visit again

Kamambo...
The butterfly hovers at the wave's lip
playing by the moorings
stopped now by the golden sun
as yellow as my mother's mat
Her scented hair fills my dreams
There is a beach
alongside the canoe

A girl clad in palm leaves
waves longingly
lining up to wait
A thousand miles of worries,
Songs of foam disappear in trees.

And, turning around
Kimi-Amang the Fantail,
calls again and again
Andev waves his banner
greetings are shared

A potion tasting as blue as the sea –
a bitter slice
of the mountains

Moody thoughts...
Why grieve?
Even wounds may be worn proudly

There, in the groove of the sand
at the tail end of one's step
he remains

How sublime
the butterfly's visit.

Hold it right there
the remaining breeze but a breath
becalmed

Anticipating the moon
as the evening drifts away
Even the butterfly rests

Is it possible she stirs?
perhaps in joy
lulled by childhood memories

O Butterfly
hovering at the lip of the wave
Wipe the oil from waiting faces
Sing the grief in blue skies,
Find happiness
as carefree as your tune.

# Antarawihi, the Magic Leaf

The mid-morning sky is cloudy. The morning's mood seems to linger. Lines of light drizzle create lines of melody, but they evaporate before hitting the surface of the water. There is no sign of activity on the beach. It is as if every living creature has decided to be silent. Andevavait is reminded of Bohurai the toadfish. All night long he had been affected by the story of Angge, the female crab. He decided that there would be no harm in visiting Bohurai, and to check up on Anggereai's family.

Oddly enough, Bohurai looked healthy in his fasting place. If anything, his stomach was looking rounder and protruded further out of the water. Seeing his friend coming, Bohurai smiled happily and greeted Andevavait. He was so fat that when he laughed you could no longer see his eyes. Andevavait understood his friend's condition and could only imagine what the consequences would be. But that was not the reason for his visit this time.

'My friend, you are fasting,' said Andevavait. 'I'm sorry I disturbed you. You aren't angry?'

'It doesn't matter, Andev, it's been ages since I saw you.'

'I came by just to see how you are.'

'Thanks, Andev. Is there something I can help you with?'

'It's about your neighbour, Anggereai.'

'What's up with him?'

'Do you know his wife, Angge?'

'Yes.'

'Do you know where she comes from?'

'I have no idea.'

'According to Anggereai, they were married at the home of her parents.'

'Just a minute, Andev. What exactly do you want to know?'

'Listen first. According to Anggereai, his wife often ate a certain leaf. As a vegetable, he said.'

'So? Is that all you came to talk about?'

'Exactly! I'm suspicious about that leaf.'

'What do you mean?'

'As if you don't know!'

'No.'

'It's called Aiwawin, the magic leaf!'

'I don't understand. What's that?'

'Oh, sorry. Indeed you probably don't know much about this. Aiwawin is the female leaf of magical attraction. But there are also male leaves, used to hypnotize the males. That's why I suspect that the female Angge was created by Anggereai.'

Bohurai the toadfish stayed still for several moments, and from his facial expression it looked as if he was seriously trying to remember something. His fin swiped at his bulging stomach several times as if he was about to scratch his armpit, but the tip couldn't reach. He finally spoke: 'What a coincidence, Andev, my friend! Lately they have often been drunk together and behaving strangely.'

'Really?'

'I once heard them fight. But then their voices were hushed. Maybe they were embarrassed to be heard by their neighbours.

They think all I do is snore.'

'So?' said Andevavait.

'When he is drunk, Anggereai always thinks his wife looks very old.'

'Did you see her?'

'I did! Actually his wife is still very young.'

'Oh.'

'I thought she looked extremely beautiful!'

Andevavait shook his head. 'Anggereai is always like that. If he gets drunk, he is out of control.'

'That's not the problem. But from a number of arguments I have heard, I don't think Anggereai is in the wrong.'

'Why?'

'It was about that wound on his wife's leg that never has healed. Yes, and you were mentioned as well!'

'Really?'

'Anggereai was very angry. He thinks that you both were nearly killed because of that wound of his wife's. And then the medicinal herbs you got were of little use.'

'But if that wound was on a young person's limb, it would surely have healed already,' Andevavait replied.

'So what do you think is the problem?'

'Have you ever seen another female at their dwelling place?'

'No.'

'I mean, an elderly female.'

'Never!'

'Besides her?'

'Besides his wife, there is no other female.'

'Not even a very elderly female?'

'I've never seen a grandmother there. Anggereai lives only with his wife.'

'Thanks, friend. That means my conclusion is right. You are right!'

'What do you mean? How am I right?'

'It must be Antarawihi,' said Andevavait. 'The magic leaf!'

'What's the difference with Aiwawin?'

'Perhaps I should explain. The female leaf, the singing leaf, the carving leaf, hunting leaves, leaves for calling the fish, and many more … All of them are part of the family of leaves known as Antarawihi.'

'Oh, I see.'

'Before you said that Anggereai and his wife mentioned me. Apart from the old wound, what else did they talk about?'

'Oh dear. If I say something, are you sure you won't be offended?'

'It doesn't matter, just tell me.'

Bohurai looked closely at Andevavait's face, and then glanced left and right, as if he was afraid someone would hear. 'They said you liked hanging around with Worri, the evil sea sprite. I mean, Anggereai told me you had even married Worri,'

Bohurai watched Andevavait's face for a reaction.

'You can believe what Anggereai said or not – it's up to you. But listen carefully. Do you know why, after so many years Anggereai has been married to that attractive young female, he still has no children?'

Bohurai shook his head.

'Because Anggereai's wife is an incarnation of the female Viami, the evil sprite of the land!'

Andevavait left without another word, leaving his friend Bohurai alone, and trembling.

# The Power of Airokung

At the time Anggereai had left Andevavait watching the feast on the beach, he had hurriedly gone back into the stone. There he saw the female Angge doing her exercises. Amazed, he watched all four sets of feet go up on tiptoe and slowly spin. Anggereai stayed still, his old wound disappearing in an instant. Now he could see the original face of his wife. Her eyes commanded him to stay put. Anggereai submitted, and sat down where he was, in front of the pile of his wife's possessions: her woven *aderi* bag, her blunt *noifa* knife and *airokung* – her betelnut crusher. Anggereai knew all of these things, and he knew there was still one more precious object inside her *aderi* bag. Her *kamoni*, a purse made of woven palm leaf, that is used for keeping special leaves with magic powers, remained inside.

Still unable to believe his eyes, Anggereai went back to watching the spinning legs. The female crab stopped exactly in front of her betelnut crusher, and her hands waved in sign language, pointing from her mouth to something inside the *airokung*. Anggereai understood the request. Without saying anything he went off in search of the requested item. The crab reached for her bag and took out her *kamoni* purse, dumping the entire contents of it on the floor. She chose several young leaves and put them into Airokung. Then she chewed up the remaining leaves. A few minutes later, she began to rub the chewed up leaves on her body. Rubbing, wiping them on her own face, her fingers then moved to her thin chest. Then she paused, took a breath, and chanted a mantra.

Anggereai reappeared, bearing an areca nut in each hand. On top of each nut balanced a betel leaf. Politely he placed the two nuts and the leaf in front of his wife. His wife directly took her *noifa* knife, peeled the nuts and placed them carefully at the bottom of the *airokung* tube. Then she added the betel leaf. Now she took a folded leaf from her basket and dropped that, too, into Airokung. Then she put the *airokung* back into her bag and tied it up. Anggereai patiently watched the entire process, and this was the part he liked best. When she was drunk, his wife had often demonstrated the power of Airokung. Now he witnessed it again. The difference now was that this time neither of them had been drinking.

They heard the distant sound of drumming. Slowly it became clearer. From the rhythm it sounded like people were dancing and beating drums, but in a little while the sound became all messed up, rhythms overlapping. And there was another sound, like the wheels of a locomotive that was moving faster and faster. Suddenly it changed again and now they could hear the sounds of a *Mandohi* feast. The *aderi* bag began to move of its own accord and the *airokung* inside swayed with it, joining in the rhythm. The female crab's mouth mumbled incoherently. Anggereai remained as still as a statue. He didn't even blink. His wife moved closer to the *aderi* purse, her mouth still uttering sounds, and she undid the bonds. Slowly she reached inside. The instant she did this the sound of the *Mandohi* retreated. Then quickly she pulled her hands out and held the mouth of the *aderi* bag tight. The sound of the *Mandohi* could once more be heard from afar. The red hands of Anggereai's wife rubbed her body. Then she slipped the *noifa* and *kamoni* back into the *aderi* bag and passed it to Anggereai.

Anggereai was about to speak, but the female held up her hand.

'Put it away!' she said.

Any doubts Anggereai might have had were dispelled by his wife's words.

'You must guard it! This is the legacy of the Wondi house!'

Anggereai thought he detected something wrong with his wife. Why had she suddenly become so strange and why was he no longer allowed to contradict her? Now he admitted, his wife seemed really very old. But what was it that made her appear so different?

Suddenly his wife commanded him again.

'Your last responsibility is to take me to the hills. Remember, only as far as the foothills. Then you may return.'

It was as if the sky had collapsed on Anggereai's head.

He felt as if he had heard a voice from the dead. But it was his wife who had spoken. Surely she must have received her orders from the afterlife. And she, his wife, would soon die.

Anggereai was struck by confusion. He felt as if he were possessed, and his body was rapidly expanding and deflating. Without further ado, his wife set out toward the hill and the final altar.

All through their journey to the foot of the hill, Anggereai moved in a daze. He danced and sang, but he couldn't see and he couldn't hear. His dance was like a statement of anger, a declaration of war on anyone who interfered with his wife, and at the same time it was a cry of anguish, full of tears that must be held back, because his wife had no choice but to go through with this. Why hadn't she told him that she would have to leave?

She knew her husband was entering a period of suffering. She knew what would happen if he had to live alone, when she finally left him. She could feel the reverberations of the screams her husband was keeping inside. He must not let it explode, because if that were to happen, there would be no blessing on her journey. All living creatures would hear the scream of her husband and that would be a disaster.

All through this night on the final altar, his wife would be introduced to the inhabitants of the universe. From different constellations, those that come out in the afternoon up until the last ones to appear in the sky. All through the night she would be honoured with stories of orange carriages that were drawn by twelve thousand flying fish, tales of seafaring boats that sailed around the earth, of people who flew from star to star, and all the famous ones who have written their whispered messages down on white paper, those who are clever at discerning the voice of water, the voices of the wind, and changing them into a hymn for all times. Even those masters who do the paintings found in thick books. They are the only ones who can approach her and shake her hand, taking turns, until just before dawn.

The male from that last star approaches her and touches her body softly. When he reaches for her hand, the female cannot refuse. 'Come on, we will go first,' he says, 'and the light will follow us!' Then he begins to dance and sing.

*Mushu phe – mushu phe; I am coming – I am coming.*

# Tentamu – Absolute Perfection

Lying in the canoe paddled by Andevavait, Bohurai the toadfish looked up at the beautiful full moon. He enjoyed the beauty of the blue sky in the middle of the night. It was strange that the night sky could be so bright. There was the moon and brightly shining stars, and yet the sky was as blue as if were the middle of the day. Now he felt free and independent. He had held out for so long, keeping to himself. He felt proud that he had atoned for his mistakes of the past. He was pleased that he had been able to help many of the scavengers. He was rightfully joyful, and he allowed his tears to fall into the water. They were tears of happiness.

Andevavait allowed the canoe to float as he watched the coral sponges below them and observed the busy nightlife in the water. The coral and the sponges were active in the night in order to multiply and grow. That was why the sound of the hustle and bustle of their growing could be heard more during the night than during the day. Bohurai turned upside down so he could see what Andevavait was up to.

'Stop a moment, Andev. Can you see it down there? That!' said Bohurai to Andevavait, pointing.

'What do you see?'

'There, the Raja's bed.'

'Which one?' asked Andevavait, doubtful.

'That's the blanket, I know the Raja's empress always wraps herself in it.'

'Oh stop it! You are still drunk, my friend.'

'I'm in perfect ... control. My friend, I have one last request!'

'What do you mean?'

'Tell me, is it the Empress I can smell?'

'No, that is the smell of an ordinary female.'

'Oh how fragrant, the throne!'

'That's the lust gland, Aroma Bia!'

'Can you tell me the name of that Bia-bia?'

'What do you mean?'

'I wish to choose one.'

'Impossible, you are not of the Mimaing tribe.'

'It's not impossible, my intuition tells me so!'

'Good, if that's the case then it's only a matter of proclaiming that you are the one. Say "*Awetandoam*; fertility is flowering between the stones!"'

'Done!' shouted Bohurai.

'*Tantemi*; flowering and full of fragrance, amongst the coral!'

'Done!' Bohurai repeated.

'*Wonai*; green, purple and delicately, intimately enticing.'

'Carry on, go on.'

'*Romang*; the giant clam at the bottom of the ocean.'

Suddenly Bohurai turned his body and sprawled out looking up at the sky, as if giving thanks. Then he groaned like an animal in agony, his voice faltering. Unable to stop himself, he turned and dived in, invading the domain of the Empress. There was nobody there. Even the Raja was gone, goodness knows where ...

Bohurai sat on the throne, the new Raja ... and then the portal closed.

He was enclosed by darkness!

And after that the only sound to be heard was the gentle 'plop!' of coconuts as they rose to the surface of the water that was glowing with the lights of the night.

Andevavait could only whisper:

'*Aro ... Anggadi tupa, anggadi tupa*! The coconuts are coming! The coconuts are coming!'

Finally morning came. After Bohurai met his untimely end behind the dark portal, Andevavait paddled his boat back to the beach. There he saw many people gathered.

Suddenly they all rushed into the water and pushed their canoes. Andevavait was nearing the beach, so he let his boat float. The sea breeze blew it ashore and eventually cast it onto the sand. At that moment, he felt hundreds of eyes were watching – there was a flock of *raheba* cruiser birds, the ones who patrol the coastline; they looked like swallows.

For his own safety, Andevavait had no choice but to dive back into his water world.

# Inov the Poisonous Stonefish

When Man understands himself as part of creation, then it's easy for him to be fair to other living things, and exist within the synergy of harmonious creation.

It is the same with all life under the sea. For example, the octopus Raukahi, who existed like a small nation-state that has always had everything it needed, had never been tempted to covet or have any power over Rawedain the fire-fish, decorated with his vibrant sparkling colours – nor, for that matter, over Nuai, the poisonous stonefish, who appeared to him to be primitive, ancient and stupid.

Whenever he likes, Raukahi's tentacles can easily wrap around the body of Nuai from eight directions. This is Raukahi we are talking about; his instincts for danger constantly honed. Even human beings, with all their common sense, will find themselves tempted by the fire-fish and the stonefish. But when recognized for what they are, in a flash the body of Rawedain or Nuai will be released, because both of them are equally poisonous. However, if the octopus forgets its instinct and lusts after Nuai (or Inov, as he is known in the Biak language), then he will increase the power of his suction until he has gripped the entire body of Inov from eight cardinal directions.

Yet Inov will not die!

As his tentacles are infected by the poison, the reckless octopus's instinctive reflex is to quickly loosen his grip. Inov will be released and Raukahi will camouflage himself to look like the reef, stretching out his poisoned tentacles and allowing them to float in the current. When this happens, Andawai the triggerfish will inevitably show up to help amputate the poisoned tips of Raukahi's tentacles.

The octopus's stumps will be painful. But he too will survive!

If the levels of poison are minimal, then Andawai will happily devour the poisoned flesh of the octopus, because this thick-skinned fish has a stronger immune system than others. In return, the triggerfish will make a hole for the octopus to hide in. Then he will advise the wounded octopus to stay in the cave until his tentacles grow back to perfection.

Only a witless octopus would disregard Andawai's advice or refuse to cooperate with him, due to their ability to help each other. These are the truly remarkable creatures that dwell at the bottom of the sea!

# Epilogue

The evening sky is clear. A grandfather sits beneath the *wawaru* beach hibiscus tree. His grandson draws near to him.

'Tete! Can you tell me? How is it trees can grow here?' he says.

'It's like this, my grandchild, the story I heard from my *cicit*,' says the old man.

'Who is your *cicit*, Tete?'

'That *cicit*? It was my grandpa's father!'

'That *cicit*, it was Tete's grandpa's father?' The child repeats this again and again.

'Tete's grandpa's father is too long. Just say, Tete's *cicit* or *tete tafu*.'

'*Tete tafu*, okay.'

'Now listen to my story. In those old days, there were no plants on this island. It was a white sandy place, surrounded by coral reefs. When they were small, my *tete tafu* told me they used to sail, together with their father and mother, far away from our village. They sailed right across the ocean. One night their canoe hit the coral reef of the island and nearly sank. Luckily, inside the coral reefs they struck were stretches of white sand. That was where their boat ran aground. When the tide went out, fish were trapped in the small pools and they could easily catch those fish. Fish became their only food.'

'In this way they were able to survive,' Tete continued. 'In the following days their boat became their home. When they were playing in the waves, my great-grandfather saw coconuts appearing in the waves. "*Anggadi tupa*," he called, "The coconuts are coming!" And dried coconuts appeared in the surf and were cast on the beach. They ran to gather them. They ate some, and the others they planted along the beach.'

'Tete, why did *tete tafu*, great-grandpa, run away from the village to the island?'

'He didn't run away. One day you will understand.'

'So where is his village?'

'One day you will know!'

There was no sign that the old man would continue the story. He just gazed at his grandson, as his thoughts wandered far into the future. The boy was impatient.

'But how could they appear out of the reef, Tete?'

'Because of *serakah* – greed. Greed cannot be hidden.'

'Who is *serakah*, Tete?'

'*Serakah* is not a person. It is only a part of a person,' said the grandfather.

'What shape is it and what does it look like?'

The old man could explain only by telling a story that showed what *serakah* meant.

'It's just like our human nature. There are those of us who like to eat lots, and never feel that they have had enough.'

The wind that blows will always blow.

Water that flows will always flow.

Dirty dust is cleaned by water.

*Dirt in the air vanishes, blown by the wind.*

The fat stored in the stomach of Bohurai the toadfish is made up of coconuts. Now his stomach has become clean. Obesity is caused by an excess of waste fat in the body.

In the realm that exists between the land and the sea the essence of feeling full, having eaten enough, is often related to the coconut tree. The stomach feels it has had enough and the brain orders the mouth to stop. When the stomach is not used to feeling replete, it will beg to be filled again and again, so there will never be a feeling of fullness or of having had enough.

When there is never any feeling of satisfaction then greed grows greater – this is *serakah!*

If it is planted and looked after, greed too will grow and bear flowers. Then it will have fruit. The fruits of greed arise of their own volition, they bear witness to greed itself. Maybe because of this, there are some villages along the coast of this bay that depict their god with a carving showing a head bigger than the body.

Just as Andevavait stores a cache of knowledge in his head that makes his head bigger than his body, the opposite effect will be achieved by depicting the god within ourselves as having a stomach that gets bigger and bigger. Images of a big belly are part of an avaricious culture that contradicts our circular existence. Everyone potentially has a large stomach like Bohurai. But the problem depends upon the owner of the stomach, and whether or not he knows how to care for it in a reasonable manner.

*Marising' tonana ya!* Be happy forever more!

# Kampong Vietnam and its historic background

*An excerpt from an article published in* Tabloid JUBI, *2009*

Kampong Vietnam, or Vietnam Village, is part of a story of the futility of war – the war that began at Pearl Harbour and ended with Hiroshima–Nagasaki. Apparently this story has never ended, having been refracted into a different timeline and another kind of battle that also shows no sign of ending.

To this day, in this particular village, it is as with the villagers of Vietnam who are still reaping the effects of the leftover landmines, even though the Vietnam War has long been over. Although this 'Kampong Vietnam' is in Papua, most of the men who live there have built their living and their family economy upon the waste munitions left over from the Pacific War. Here the non-proliferation treaty – and other similar treaties regarding leftover landmines and sea mines or even warheads – has no meaning. In Kampong Vietnam there are no spoils of war or rehabilitation for the losers, crippled or dead.

The name 'Kampong Vietnam' originated from the disastrous exploding handmade bombs that continue to take victims' lives or cripple them. It has become commonplace to see people from Kampong Vietnam who are maimed and crippled, like the war casualties of mainland Vietnam. Nobody knows exactly when the village first earned this reputation; however, they say it is the similarity between victims and their stories of leftover landmines from the Vietnam War that started it.

A fishing village at Argapura Beach in the sub-district of South Jayapura in Papua originated with Jayapura government policy at the beginning of the 1970s. At that time the government was trying to clean up the slums around the city centre and port. Accordingly, with the agreement of the traditional Kayu Polo organization (a branch of the Ondoafi[1] royal confederation), the settlement in Weerf (now situated behind Bekang), was moved to Argapura Beach or Klapperland, as it was known in Dutch times.

The problem then arose as to why the people of the fishing village – originally the designated community to supply fish to the city of Jayapura and now already in their second and third generation – chose to use bombs and explosives as a practical way to increase their catch. Why did the government not make an effort to stop them using the remnants of a war as a means of survival? Why did they not 'learn their lesson', instead of becoming more reckless – in spite of the terrible consequences that could happen at any time and which they had observed again and again with their own eyes? Why did the government no longer stick to its policies of policing and limiting new migrant settlers, for which they had initially cleared away the fishing village, leaving Weerf clean and tidy? Instead, they allowed the area to revert back to slums, crowded with seedy shacks.

Why were the traditional authorities and government not able to police the fishing community from Kosong Island, simply

---

1. The Ondoafi region includes a number of tribal areas around Lake Sentani. The villages included are situated in five regions: Asei, Ayapo, Yoka, Waena and Asei.

as a part of enforcing city regulations? And how did the fishing industry of the local people then pass into the hands of the newly arrived migrant communities from Buton and Makassar?

These questions and their reality are difficult to answer. However, the important thing is to review the problems that have arisen one by one, over the long process of a century of 'advanced' civilization having penetrated this bay.

Half a century before this, on April 22, 1944 to be exact, the Allied Forces won Red Beach Bay, Tanah Merah Bay, and Hollandia back from the occupying Japanese forces. Through the efforts of the Reckless Task Force, a single army corps commanded by Lieutenant General Robert L. Eichelberger and the Alamo Force (Sixth US Army) under the command of Lieutenant General Walter Krueger, the commander of Infantry division 24 Mayor General Frederick Irving, the commander of division 41 Mayor General Horace Fuller, and General Douglas MacArthur and his forces, they took them back one by one with their leapfrog strategy.

After Hollandia, Biak, Morotai, Saipan and Iwo Jima, Okinawa soon followed. Then the atom bombs ended the war in the Pacific at Hiroshima and Nagasaki, on August 6 and 9, 1945. The regions of Humboldt Bay, along with Tanah Merah Bay, had been secured on June 6, 1944, and Hollandia was developed into Base G, housing the main strength of the Allied forces in the Pacific. Papua was the headquarters of the United States Army for the Southwest Pacific, the United States Army in the Far East, the Air Force of the Allied forces, the Army of the Allied Forces, the 7th Fleet of the USA, the 5th Fleet Air Force, the Allied Air Force, the ground battalions of the Allied Forces, the 7th US Armada, the 5th Air force Armada, the Alamo Task Force (6th US Army) and 8th Armada Army.[2]

Once the Pacific War was over, the Allies returned sovereignty over New Guinea to the Dutch, and the town of Hollandia was prepared to be the provincial capital and centre of administration, with all the necessary infrastructure.

In organizing the postwar government, the first governor, S.L.J. van Waardenburg, issued a resolution, (no. 43), dated June 14, 1950, that revoked the decision of the Dutch East Indies Government of July 13, 1945 and January 14, 1949 regarding the status of Nieuw Guinea as a '*neolandschap*' area. According to *Besluit Bewindsregeling Nieuw-Guinea*, the Queen of Holland officially revoked this status from June 1, 1950 onward, with the appointment of the Governor of Nederland Nieuw Guinea. The statutes of governance thereof became the new parliamentary rules for the area that would formulate the rights of the people of New Guinea.[3]

In building the physical infrastructure of Hollandia, during the third period of Governor S.L.J. van Waardenburg, Jan van Baal, and Pieter J. Platteel (1950 to 1962), four contracting companies were appointed: Ballast Maatschappij were in charge of roads; Hollandsche Betton Maatschappij (HBM) were placed in charge of bridges; Intervaam Maatschappij of housing; and Bawm Maatshappij of hospitals. Before those contractors could carry out any work, the recruitment and the work force needed to

---

2. *MacArthur Museum/Monument*
3. *JRG Djopari pp. 26-27*

be trained in advance by NV Sentani/Maskapai Sentani.

A large number of these workers were brought in from Serui and Biak. They were accommodated at Arbeiders Camp, a worker's camp that consisted of sixteen round barracks set up in the Weerf district. At the same time, Onderafdeeling Hollandia issued a regulation restricting settlers. This rule was meant to anticipate an explosion of urbanization in the town, which was developing very fast. Every person who arrived for the first time in Hollandia had to register. If they did not have a work contract with the authorities, or one of the four contractors above, they were sent directly home.

In consideration of the length of the contract and the workers' background as seafaring people, the government of Hollandia and the Kayu Pulo traditional community agreed that the workers, who mostly came from the kampong of Ambai (Serui people), would be allowed to build houses in the Weerf area.

This was not the case for educated workers. Formal employees placed in companies and offices were provided the same facilities as government employees, according to their position and job, and housed in elite housing complexes such as Dok V, Dok VII, Dok VIII and Dok IX. Moreover, to prevent social jealousy or internal conflict between the traditional seafaring people, a fishing cooperative was formed known as Hena Tadje, directly under the supervision of the Resident of Hollandia, without any village chief or interim body. The job of the cooperative was to look after the fishermen and their catch, including setting the limits of the fishing area for those who used the modern system of fishing and outboard motor boats.

Why then, after independence, when Papua reverted to the civil government of Indonesia, did the people in this village begin to adopt a method of fishing that is not allowed at all by the legal code? They still tend to justify themselves in this action, which has proven destructive to both themselves and their environment, destroying the coral reefs and the marine ecosystem. Could this anomaly represent some kind of rebellious protest against injustice? But then again, surely it offered a potential threat to collective harmony, regardless of the original purpose and function of the weapons, if they should become directed toward some kind of protest or resistance. This fear is plausible and rational – the act of recycling the products of war is no empty gesture. On the other hand, even on a small scale, this action of civil disobedience has caused victims. Along with the name 'Kampong Vietnam' has appeared a kind of psychological illness, one that the fishing village community has not found any medicine to heal. This acute illness could perhaps be described as the 'Crazy Bomb Syndrome'. It seems incurable; even the government has failed to address it.

The Vietnam Village has also proliferated, so that we now have Kampong Vietnam II, III, and IV, the latter being situated within the Navy complex, Lantamal X Papua.

It is difficult to improve the atmosphere and conditions in Papua in the midst of uncertainty, although many circles boast that Papua is a now a 'peaceful region'. A century ago, when the gospel was brought to the Humboldt Bay by the Dutch evangelists Ev. Bijkerk, Ev. Scheider and Ev. De Neef, it seemed to them that the Tabi people of Papua were still at war, killing each other. And right up until a century later, with the advent of a 'globally integrated society', the seeds of war are still at large. So should we remain cautious? The image of the Papuans as a people who like to make war remains and continues to be preserved and cultivated.

How can we put the Papuan people and their problems into a coconut shell, while the ringing spirit of 'peace on earth' in this region has been echoing ever since General Douglas MacArthur, way back on August 15, 1945, pledged peace in Hollandia? The context of declaring peace in Papua today is in no way narrow or local. In Indonesia the level of threat of conflict is rated similarly to that in Sampit or Poso, for example, locations famous as hot beds of terrorism.

A fundamental question arises: Who should be responsible for the leftover war munitions in this region?

The region was undeniably a part of World War II. Should America and Japan be held responsible? Or should the Allied Forces? Is the recycling of warheads left over from the war in the Pacific not considered to be some kind of proliferation? Should Indonesia not be involved and join in the ratification of the non-proliferation treaty at an international level?

Indeed, discussing one hundred years of Hollandia is not as easy as bragging about the successes of reaching the top of an ivory tower. While we are occupied with shouting out the successes of progress, at our feet remain strewn decades of very real destruction, albeit in rather elegant and festive variety.

\*) Excerpts from an article that was published in *Tabloid JUBI*, at the end of 2009 as part of 'Review: 100 years of Jayapura city.'

# *Sapuriwan*

(Original poem in Ambai language, from page 162.)

Sapuriwan
Mana wero?
simana wero marutu e ..
Rawa wa wesau tenggare
Sirire siriwa mawa e
Inenerya ronda rame puyo
Kowoi ya ayawa rome
Menewe wapa sapu riwani.


Mana wero simana wero
Apakara diani marutu nie..
Sirire siriwa mawa e ..
Amene imbori ronda ramera

# Glossary of Ambai Words

This glossary of words about the sea from the Ambai language is taken from just one of the many local languages from the inhabitants of the Saireri (Austronesian) region, which includes Geelvink Bay and Cendrawasih Bay areas in the northern regions of the main island of Papua.

This tribe has not only a glossary of words for various underwater species, but it also maintains references to the relationships between those species, depicting their mutual symbiosis. Although the 'law of the jungle' still applies here, the natural balance remains, due to the ability of our people to still appreciate the connectivity of life in a single dimension, that dimension where humans, animals and plants exist together. In many portraits of underwater life, the people of Ambai from the thousands of islands of Papua take their responsibility seriously: to reflect upon and discover the meaning of each traditional teaching, according to their way of life and choice of profession.

| | |
|---|---|
| Aderi | a traditional woven bag. |
| Afura | a species of white dove. |
| Aidorehi | *Tambelo Batu*, a type of worm that lives in the mangroves. |
| Aifa | *karaka*, a large crab that lives in the mangrove forest. |
| Aii | mother. |
| Ainai | Endracht hardyhead, Lat. *Atherinomorus endrachtensis*. |

| | |
|---|---|
| Aindori | a kind of catfish (Ikan Sembilang) that live in the mixed fresh water and seawater where the mangrove forest grows Ai-reng the lip of the beach where the sea meets the sand. |
| Airokung | a tool for pounding betel nut. |
| Aiwa | Queensland or giant grouper, Lat. *Epinephelus lanceolatus*. |
| Aiwawin | a type of leaf used for black magic/to attract the opposite sex. |
| Aiweirori | flower crabs, Lat. *Portunus pelagicus*. |
| Amaren | a freshwater eel that lives in the mangrove forest or river. |
| Ampaiso | White Crane (Ind. Bangau Putih), Lat. *Ciconia ciconia*. |
| Ampam-purem | small fish that like to pose, and live in groups on the reef. |
| Ampar | the morning star |
| Amperung | Crescent Perch, Lat. *Terapon jarbua*. |
| Ampite | Bird-lime Tree, Lat. *Pisonia umbellifera*. (bark used to treat Diabetes) |
| Amumar | Moon Wrasse, Lat. *Thalassoma lunare*. |
| Andawai | red-lined triggerfish, Lat. *Balistapus undulates*. |
| Andevavait | spotted tidepool blenny, Lat. *Istiblennius meleagris* an amphibious fish. |
| Anggadi | coconut / coconut palm. |
| Anggadi Tupa | a mature coconut that floats upon the surface of the water. |
| Anggarariti | term used for any type of crab / crab family. |
| Anggereai | an amphibious crab. He lives in the rocks at the seaside. This crab has a thin and skinny body but it is able to cling on to the rocks in strong currents and smashing waves. Sometimes it is found on logs that have been carried by current out to sea. |
| Anina | a small bird with black feathers and red eyes. It lives in big groups. |
| Aniowa | a turtle, of any kind |
| Anotar | snakehead murrel, Lat. *Channa striata*. |
| Ansanai | a Flat-tailed Longtom Lat. *Platybelone platyura*. |
| Ansansina | Sea Urchin, Lat. *Echinus melo*. |

| | |
|---|---|
| Antanai | bareback anchovy, Lat. *Papuengraulis micropinna Munro*. |
| Antarawihi | a type of leaf believed to provide magical protection/magical powers. |
| Arawi | a type of hawk. |
| Are-metang | Golden-lined Spinefoot, Ind. Ikan samandar-papan, Lat. *Siganus lineatus*. |
| Aringgoya | a spear-gun made out of bamboo and thick wire |
| Arireni | a type of wide-leafed bamboo normally used to wrap cassava. |
| Aroang | threadfin emperor fish, Lat. *Lethrinus genivittatus*. |
| Atho | arrow. |
| Athohuri | special bamboo used to make arrows. |
| Aumpe | a type of bamboo with long segments used to keep water in. |
| Awaha | stars in the sky. |
| Awaingge | grey heron, often called the beach heron. |
| Awesuain | Grouper, Lat. *Cephalopholis sp*. |
| Awetandoam | a species of Bia Garo/mollusc that lives in cracks of the rocks. |
| Awohoi | cigarettes or tobacco. |
| Awohoi-kumu | compacted tobacco that is held between gum and lips and sucked. |
| Ayadiru | a bat, Ind. kelelawar/paniki |
| Bitau | Bitanggur tree, (Milkwood tree) |
| Bitowai | Butterfly fish, Lat. *Chaetodon sp*. |
| Bohurai | Stars and Stripes toadfish/Pufferfish, Lat. *Arothron hispidus* |
| Bompai | Owl, Ind. Burung Hantu |
| Bui | a carving motif that contains symbols of particular significance. |
| Daii | Father, Dad. A term also used for a respected person or elder. |
| Dediru | night, also known as 'Meti malam'. |
| Diang | a term for all species of fish. |
| Diario | Dugong, called sea cows, becoming increasingly rare in Papua. |
| Dobaraia | storm or hurricane. |
| Embai | moon. |

| | |
|---|---|
| Embatang | Dash-Dot Goatfish, Lat. *Parupeneus barberinus*. |
| Fafuta | another species of seaweed. |
| Faiya | a small carry bag made of woven palm leaf, used to carry clothes and valuables. |
| Fakihing | a species of brown-coloured seaweed. |
| Farah | a species of solid, rounded seaweed with small leaves that grows in sandy and rocky areas |
| Farai | mangrove tree/mangrove forest. |
| Fawei | a species of crab that lives in the same habitat as Aiweirori. |
| Fayamai | a type of bamboo used as a knife or Kalawai. |
| Fimuna | Cuscus, Ind. Kus-kus, the shy Polecat/Loris. |
| Fodamir | Striped Catfish, Lat. *Plotosus lineatus*. |
| Fuina | year. |
| Fuina/saya fuina | low tide season, Indonesian: Musim meti siang/musim surut. |
| Furuhi | a species of shellfish that live in the mangroves. |
| Gorano | Stone fish, has poisonous spikes, Ind. Ikan Batu, Lat. *Synanceia verrucosa.* |
| Gutila | Sailfin Surgeonfish, or Ringed Tang, Lat. *Zebrasoma veliferum*. |
| Jarabonia | Blue-spotted stingray. |
| Je Anggadi | known as Saguer beverage or palm wine, Indonesian: tuak (fermented sap from the coconut palm). |
| Je Vereng | known as 'Sleepy drink', a nipah palm-wine. |
| Kadoi | a beach almond tree growing near the seashore which bears edible nuts. Indonesian: Pohon ketapang. |
| Kafoni | White-chested Red Eagle. |
| Kaintani | kingfisher, Ind. Burung raja udang. |
| Kamambo | Butterfly. |
| Kamantifu | Monitor lizard. |
| Kambutir | Split-banded cardinalfish, Lat. *Apogon compessus*. |
| Kambuwir | a traditional harpoon weapon made of bamboo/steel, Indonesian: Sumpit. |
| Kambuwir | Smooth Flutemouth, Lat. *Fistularia commersonil*. |
| Kamoni | a purse made of woven palm leaf. |
| Kara | a species of white cockatoo. |

| | |
|---|---|
| Karani | a labour recruiter. |
| Karatar | jellyfish. |
| Karu | a species of seaside tree. |
| Karu | mouse. |
| Kawawori | a seaside tree with leaves used to make mats. |
| Kawein | a term for any kind of shrimp, or lobster. |
| Kencumi/ | a type of seaweed that has a fibrous stem, used to make a natural thread for kusumi traditional fishing nets. |
| Kerephuni | Sharp-Nosed Wrasse, Lat. *Cheilio inermis*. |
| Ketapang | a tropical Sea Almond tree of the leadwood family, Lat. *Terminalia catappa*. |
| Kikou | Black-spot sea perch, Lat. *Lutjanus fulvilflamma*. |
| Kimi-amang | Mangrove Fantail, Ind. Burung Kris Ekor Kipas, Lat. *Rhipidura phasiana*. |
| Kirikoni | King Cockatoo/Palm Cockatoo, Ind. Kakatua Raja, Lat. *Probosciger aterrimus*. |
| Koisepa/Rouw | a raft. |
| Konggomirai | a family of molluscs, the shell of which is often used by octopus as a shelter/shield when swimming, or crossing from one point to another. |
| Korowei | a species of Hawk. |
| Kowar | Whitley's sergeant. Ind. Ikan baju kos, Lat. *Abudefduf whitleyi*. |
| Kumu | tobacco. |
| Kutte | a mollusc that lives in the mangroves Lat. *Bactrohophorus thoracites*. |
| Mambara | a species of yellow turtle. |
| Mambara-kamiai | Brown-banded cat-shark, Lat. *Chiloscyllium punctatum*. |
| Mamboasar | seahorse, Ind. Kuda laut, Lat. *Hippocampus*. |
| Mamurang | a large Bamboo, Ind. Bambu petung, Lat. *Dendrocalamus asper*. |
| Manderi | a species of mangrove, the trunk of which is used as an outrigger. |
| mandohai | a general term for sharks |
| Mandohi | a dance party |
| Mandong | a species of seaweed used to make traditional fishing nets. |
| Manggeng | Seagull, Ind. Burung camar. |

| | |
|---|---|
| Manggio | partridge/pheasant. |
| Manggofuni | Grasshopper/Locust, Ind. Belalang. |
| Mansoari | Cassowary, Ind. Burung Kasuari, Lat. Fam. *Casuariidae*. |
| Mansomunu | a type of locust that uses its long hands as weapons. |
| Mantei | who. |
| Mantemboni | fruit of a seaweed, Ind. buah mandong. |
| Manunggarum | a species of seaweed that grows in sandy areas. The roots are sweet, and it is a favourite food for dugong (sea cows). |
| Maradea | Grouper, Lat: *Epinephelus*. |
| Maraiberar | Tripletail Maori Wrasse, Lat. *Cheilinus trilobatus*. |
| Marang | species of tree used to make Tifa drums. |
| Marirori | shady, calm, describes the calm surface of the ocean. |
| Mori/moridai | smudgespot Spinefoot, *Siganus canaliculatus*. |
| Muantonang | Thumbprint Emperor, Lat. *Lethrinus harak*. |
| Muntung | Great pigeon, or Pinon imperial pigeon; Ind. Burung kum-kum kelang. |
| Nafabua | a white sand beach. |
| Nanna | Sea Lettuce, also known as Beach Morning Glory, has white flowers a medicinal anti-inflammatory/relaxant leaf (edible) and the bushes prevent sand erosion; Ind. Obat luka, Lat. *Scaevola taccada*. |
| Nibon | Nibung, Lat. *Oncospermatigilarium*. |
| Noi | knife. |
| Noifa | blunt knife. |
| Noken | a knotted or woven bag which is hung from the head against the back and is traditionally used to carry various goods, and also children. |
| Novi | coconut shell. |
| Nuai | Scorpion fish, one of the world's most venomous species and a master of camouflage; Ind. ikan kalajengking. |
| Nyawaiker | Wrasse, *Lat. Halichoeres sp*. |
| Patora | a species of swallow famous for its edible birds nests; Ind. Burung Walet/Burung laying-layang. |

| | |
|---|---|
| Porobibi | Toad-fish or Puffer fish, (Bohurai the Porobibi). |
| Raimuna | a departed spirit. |
| Randumi | moss / algae. |
| Raukahi | octopus. |
| Rawedain | Spotless Firefish, Lat. *Pterois russelli*. |
| Rawei | Crow / Raven; Ind. Burung gagak. |
| Reti | a piece of wire used to catch octopus and fish. |
| Rohai | Mantis shrimp, a type of shrimp that lives and makes holes in the sand. Used as a weapon, its sharp and spiky maxillaped can kill the fish that pass its hole; Lat. *Harpiosquilla rapax*. |
| Romang | a giant mollusc that lives in the deep ocean floor. |
| Rong | Merbau wood, Lat. Intsia pelembanica. |
| Rouw/Koisepa | raft. |
| Samandar | Rabbit fish / Spinefoot, Lat. Fam. *Siganidae*. |
| Saya | night-time, during the low tide season (July December). |
| Saya fuina | day-time during the low tide season (January-June). |
| Seimumung | to talk, pronounce, protest or sulk (mutter) in an unclear manner. |
| Sera-mambiti | Raja fish or Skate, flat-bodied, cartilaginous fish with a rhombic shape; Lat. *Rajidae* |
| Sifo | Fly (Sifo na ai-reng – a fly at the edge of the water) |
| Tabeawa | Orbicular Batfish, Lat. *Platax orbicularis* |
| Tafu | Grandfather/Grandmother. Note: Tafu, Daii or Aii are also used by a mother to call her child if she recognizes in that child certain traits of the ancestor's charisma or a similar character. |
| Tantemi | a species of shell/mollusc that live in the gaps of the rocks that can swim and migrate. |
| Tarubain | highfin grouper, Lat. *Epinephelus maculatus*. |
| Tawaiseng | hookjaw moray eel, Lat. *Enchelycore bayeri*. |
| Tawawang | a seaside plant with wide leaves often used to wrap and roast sago. |
| Tentamu | perfection (a term used to describe when two ends of circular-shaped fishing nets meet exactly in the middle – e.g. a perfect cast of the net). |
| Tete | grandfather. |

| | |
|---|---|
| Titiwir | Treeshrew, Ind. tupai. |
| Tupa | to rise / emerge / surface (from the water). |
| Ubo-kahoi | Giant Herring, Lat. *Elops hawaiiensis Regan*. |
| Umahi | Hermit Crab. |
| Umbe | a big cleaver. |
| Umbehoi | a blunt cleaver. |
| Uneng | Yellow-Lined Seaperch, Lat. *Lutjanus rufolineatus*. |
| Urewang | a black and white striped sea snake. |
| Viami | genie / a spirit that rules the land. |
| Viawera | a wild dog. |
| Vitararari | Queensland Halibut, Lat. *Psettodes erumei*. |
| Vitatawin | Sea Cucumbers, Lat. *Holothuroidea*. |
| Viwaradi | Monitor lizard; Ind. Biawak. |
| Wainari | Lingua tree – Lingua sap is used as glue on Tifa drum surfaces. |
| Wanamba | The East wind. |
| Wanampui | The North wind. |
| Wanang-murang | The West wind. |
| Wanangsai | The South wind. |
| Wari | Barracuda, Lat. *Sphyraena barracuda*. |
| Wawaru | Beach Hibiscus tree. |
| We-dobarai | rolling thunder from a storm or typhoon. |
| Wiwin-tanggi | Frog/toad. |
| Wofai/Wohi | Flyingfish, Lat. *Cypselurus sp*. |
| Wohere | Termites. |
| Wonai | a species of shell/mollusc that live in the gaps of the rocks/reef. |
| Worar | Ink fruit tree. |
| Woriawa | Blue-Ringed Angelfish, Lat. *Pomacanthus annularis*. |
| Worri | Genie/Spirit of the ocean. |

# In Remembrance of the Bomb Victims
# (1970 – 2009)

**Samuel Jowey & Agustinus Jowey (fishermen) and**
**Zeth Jowey (student)**
One Sunday morning in 1970, Samuel Jowey and family were breaking open munitions found at Tanjung Marine in Hamadi when the shells exploded. All three died, their bodies shattered and burned beyond recognition.

**Eduard Maay (fisherman)**
On the afternoon of December 31, 1973, at Shipwreck, Dok II, Edu Maay was breaking open armaments on the deck of Dok II (now in front of the governor's office) when they detonated. He died instantly.

**Mas Joko (a Marine from the Navy Base at Hamadi)**
On a Sunday afternoon in 1974, Mas Joko died instantly, his body charred and full of smoking holes, after the ordnance that he was breaking apart blew up.

**La Domi (fisherman)**
After two accidents in which he lost his left arm and his right arm, La Domi finally died at sea, in Humboldt Bay, in his third and last accident when he set off a bomb that he had made himself.

**Mohamad Ali Numberi (fisherman)**
On a Sunday morning, in 1987, next to the Immanuel Church in Hamadi, an explosion at the house of Ali's father-in-law while working on a fishing bomb. He died at the emergency unit of the public hospital.

**Dance & Daniel Patai (fisherman and ex-athlete in the National Rowing Team)**
At his home in Kampung Vietnam, Argapura Pantai, in 1997, Dance Patai was with his son Daniel, splitting the head of a shell when it exploded. Dance Patai died instantly. His son, Daniel Patai, Junior swimming champion of Papua, lost both his legs. (In February 2011, Daniel Patai was still carrying on the profession of his late father, making fishing bombs.)

**Daniel Wanggai (fisherman)**
In Humboldt Bay a fishing bomb exploded and Daniel lost both his arms. He still fishes, only now he uses an outboard motor.

**Oktovianus Kareni (fisherman)**
One Sunday morning at the Kampong Vietnam in Argapura, Okto died after the head of some munitions exploded while he was cracking it open at his home.

**Warisal (husband & wife), Kali Hanyaan, Entrop**
This couple died together in the same accident as Oktovianus Kareni. The shell was taken from Tanjung Marine to Kali Hanyaan Entrop, where it exploded.

**Marthen Rumabar** (fisherman)
At Hamadi Vaambem, Kampong Vietnam III, 2001, Marthen died at home when ordnance exploded.

**Oskar Haradiani** (fisherman)
At Tanjung Marine, Hamadi, in 2000, Oskar was racing with the fish, when the bomb he had assembled exploded. His boat sank, and after twelve hours his friend Nelson Waimbo found the body caught in the coral.

**Victor Yansenem** (fisherman)
At Tanjung Marine, Hamadi, in 2003 Victor lost both legs and his left arm after the live ordnance he was working on exploded. Now, every Sunday, Victor attends church in a wheelchair, and prays to the same God that guides the soldiers in the Solomon Islands. He is the one who pinned the golden crown Anggadi Novi on the head of the President of the Scouts, USA.

**Gayus Awarawi alias Samurai** (fisherman), Pulau Anus, Sarmi, 2007
Chasing a large catch all the way to Anus Island, Gayus lost his left eye and three fingers in an explosion, as he could not move as fast as the bomb he had assembled himself.

**La Ulu** (fisherman), in the waters of Tanjung Skouw
Perhaps due to over-confidence, La Ulu was too slow, and the dynamite exploded directly in his hand. One arm was donated to the sea, in retribution.

**Panus Sibi (fisherman) in the waters of the Humboldt Bay**
As with La Ulu, Panus could not compete with the speed of the dynamite fuse. He lost an arm, which he donated to his ancestors, as it was no longer any use in defending his village.

**Tridom Muabuai (fisherman) in the waters of the Humboldt Bay**
Tridom met the same fate as La Ulu and Panus, and remains disabled until today.

**Jowel Jowir Wanggai (fisherman)**
On a Sunday morning, on the water near Pasir Dua Beach, in December 2007, while his fellow villagers were at prayer, Jowir died and drowned when the bomb he had built himself exploded in his hands.

**Jordan Rahmaon Mara (hotel security officer & fisherman)**
On the night of December 31, 2008, at the Kampong Vietnam in Argapura, struck by the thunderous clap of a dynamite detonation, Rahmaon's body exploded into the New Year.

**Yahya Karubaba (fisherman)**
Yahya had already lost his right arm in a similar accident in 1985. In June 2009, as if it was a night at the Theater Arena, Yahya died in the water at Kampong Vietnam, in front of a large audience.

OTHER VICTIMS THAT DIED IN ACCIDENTS WHILE RETRIEVING MUNITIONS FROM THE SEA (1979 – 2008)

**Bob Haay, Marthen Jowey, Elieser Patai and Achon Wanggai (all fishermen)**
In the waters at various places in Humboldt Bay, these four men all died at different times from the same cause: they ran out of oxygen while diving and were unable to reach the surface of the water in time.

# Books by Indonesian authors

### FICTION
*Cigarette Girl* by Ratih Kumala
*Harvesting the Storm* by John Waromi
*Not a Virgin* by Nuril Basri

### NONFICTION
*Jakarta Undercover* by Moammar Emka
*Jakarta Undercover II* by Moammar Emka

# Books set in Indonesia

### FICTION
*Island of Demons* by Nigel Barley
*Island Secrets* by Alwin Blum
*Mataram* by Tony Reid
*Olivia & Sophia* by Rosie Milne
*Shaman of Bali* by John Greet
*Snow over Surabaya* by Nigel Barley
*Twilight in Kuta* by David Nesbit

### NONFICTION
*Bali Raw* by Malcolm Scott
*Bali Undercover* by Malcolm Scott
*Bandit Saints of Java* by George Quinn
*In the Footsteps of Stamford Raffles* by Nigel Barley
*Raffles and the British Invasion of Java* by Tim Hannigan
*Toraja* by Nigel Barley
*You'll Die in Singapore* by Charles McCormac